THE
ROMAN
QUESTS

RETURN TO ROME

Also by Caroline Lawrence

THE ROMAN QUESTS
Escape from Rome
The Archers of Isca
Death in the Arena

THE ROMAN MYSTERIES
I The Thieves of Ostia
II The Secrets of Vesuvius
III The Pirates of Pompeii
IV The Assassins of Rome
V The Dolphins of Laurentum
VI The Twelve Tasks of Flavia Gemina
VII The Enemies of Jupiter
VIII The Gladiators from Capua
IX The Colossus of Rhodes
X The Fugitive from Corinth
XI The Sirens of Surrentum
XII The Charioteer of Delphi
XIII The Slave girl from Jerusalem
XIV The Beggar of Volubilis
XV The Scribes from Alexandria
XVI The Prophet from Ephesus
XVII The Man from Pomegranate Street

Trimalchio's Feast and Other Mini-mysteries
The Legionary from Londinium and Other Mini-mysteries

THE ROMAN MYSTERY SCROLLS
The Sewer Demon
The Poisoned Honey Cake
The Thunder Omen
The Two-faced God

THE P.K. PINKERTON MYSTERIES
The Case of the Deadly Desperados
The Case of the Good-looking Corpse
The Case of the Pistol-packing Widows
The Case of the Bogus Detective

THE ROMAN QUESTS

RETURN TO ROME

Caroline Lawrence

Orion
Children's Books

ORION CHILDREN'S BOOKS

First published in Great Britain in 2018
by Hodder and Stoughton

1 3 5 7 9 10 8 6 4 2

A CIP catalogue record for this book
is available from the British Library.

ISBN 978 1 5101 0033 6

Typeset by Input Data Services Ltd, Somerset

Printed and bound in Great Britain by Clays Ltd, St Ives plc

The paper and board used in this book are from well-managed forests
and other responsible sources.

Orion Children's Books
An imprint of
Hachette Children's Group
Part of Hodder and Stoughton
Carmelite House
50 Victoria Embankment
London EC4Y 0DZ

An Hachette UK Company
www.hachette.co.uk
www.orionchildrensbooks.co.uk

For glassmaker Stephen Pollock-Hill, who suggested I use the Minerva cameo in one of my books, and equally for his wife Sami, my gracious sister-in-law

BRITANNIA

VERULAMIUM   CAMULODUNUM   GERMANIA
LONDINIUM   INFERIOR

COLONIA CLAUDIA ARA
AGRIPPINENSIUM

GESORIACUM

GALLIA
BELGICA

GERMANIA
MAGNA

GALLIA
LUGDUNENSIS

GERMANIA
SUPERIOR

RAETIA

NORICUM

LUGDUNUM

ITALIA

PANNONIA

GALLIA
NARBONENSIS

DALMATIA

NEMAUSUS

HISPANIA
TARRACONENSIS

N

W   E

ROME
OSTIA

S

MARE INTERNUM

- - - - - -   ROUTE OF THE QUESTERS

∿∿∿∿∿∿   BORDER OF THE EMPIRE

WESTERN ROMAN PROVINCES c. AD 96

Salve (hello)!

Welcome to the fourth and final Roman Quest.

This story takes place in various provinces of the Roman Empire in the spring and summer of 96 AD, during the reign of the Emperor Domitian.

Some of the events in this book are true and most of the places are real. You can still find Roman remains and artefacts in *Verulamium* (St Albans, UK), *Gesoriacum* (Boulogne-sur-Mer, France), *Colonia Claudia Ara Agrippinensium* (Cologne, Germany), *Nemausus* (Nîmes, France), *Ostia* (Ostia Antica, Italy) and of course Rome, the 'Eternal City'. To learn more about the Emperor Domitian, start by reading the biography written by Suetonius, an eyewitness of his reign.

Most of my chapter headers are in Latin, and refer to something in that chapter. See if you can guess what the Latin words mean. Then turn to page 225 to see if you were right.

Vale (farewell)!

Caroline

I

PROLOGUS

The little girl in the tartan tunic was running for her life.

Six-year-old Bouda was the youngest cutpurse in Tyranus's gang. She was used to fleeing from the people she robbed. But on this foggy winter day in the docks of Londinium she was running from two Roman soldiers.

Their hobnail boots clattered on the wooden wharf as they chased her around oak barrels of beer from Germania, past amphoras of olive oil from Galatia and between crates of Samian ware from Gaul.

Bouda knew the docks of Londinium like a rabbit knows its warren.

But the soldiers were bigger and faster.

What would they do with her when they caught her? Would they beat her? Imprison her? Crucify her?

Her bare feet thudded faster than her heart and her red hair flew out behind her.

Bouda was proud of her hair and liked to leave it unpinned. Tyranus said it was like a flame in the fog.

It was foggy now, and in a world of white her shining copper locks might get her killed.

Behind her a clatter of armour told her one of the soldiers had slipped and fallen on to the wet planks.

As the other soldier stopped to help him, Bouda darted underneath an unhitched wagon.

Crouching in the murky light, she shrank back against one of the wheels and waited for the soldiers to hurry past. But instead of running on they stopped right beside her hiding place.

She could see the hems of their red woollen tunics, their bare legs, their boots and the tips of their swords.

'Jupiter's eyebrows!' panted the one with hairy calves. 'Where's she gone?'

'I think she went into that warehouse,' gasped the one with the bumpy knees.

'Impossible! It's too far away and the door is closed. She was right in front of me, almost within arm's reach!'

'Why are we chasing her anyway?' The wagon creaked as one of the soldiers leaned against it. 'I mean, I know she runs with that gang of cutpurses, but she's only a little girl. It's humiliating.'

'What's humiliating is that she got away,' muttered his companion. Then he lowered his voice even further. 'There's a rumour she's Boudica's great-granddaughter.'

Underneath the wagon, the little girl's eyes grew wide. Her boss Tyranus often told her she was descended from the famous red-haired warrior queen named Boudica. But whenever she told the older children they never believed her.

'Boudica's granddaughter? Hah!' scoffed the soldier with bumpy knees. 'I'll bet they say that about every red-headed girl here in Britannia.'

'Apparently this one is legitimate. They say one of Boudica's daughters died giving birth to a baby girl. The soldiers of the Second Augusta gave the baby a ring to show that one of them was the father. That daughter grew up wild and when she in turn had a baby, she abandoned the infant with nothing but the swaddling

4

bands she was wrapped in and her grandfather's ring.'

Little Bouda glanced down at the ring on her thumb. The stone was the same reddish orange as her hair. Carved into it was a tiny creature with a goat's body and a fish's tail: a Capricorn. Did it really prove she was Boudica's descendant?

'Even if she is Boudica's great-granddaughter, why does the governor want her?'

'It's not the governor who wants her. It's Domitian.'

Bouda's green eyes grew wider. Domitian was the Emperor of Rome. Everybody knew that.

'It's been nearly forty years since Boudica burnt Londinium in her rebellion against us Romans,' said Bumpy Knees. 'But it's risen from the ashes like a phoenix. Nobody cares about Boudica any more, much less her great-granddaughter.'

'Domitian does. He hasn't been doing well in his wars recently. Remember how he dressed up some slaves as Germans for his first triumph and everybody laughed at him? He needs a good show of power.'

'And you think a little girl will do it for him?'

'Yeah. I reckon he'll parade her through the streets of Rome and then publicly execute her.'

Bouda's throat was suddenly dry. She longed to visit Rome, which Tyranus often praised, but not if it meant a parade that ended in her execution.

Shivering, she shrank back against the wooden wheel of the cart.

Suddenly an arm darted through the spokes and hooked her waist. Before she could scream, a cold hand clamped over her mouth.

After a moment of pure terror, she relaxed. It was a boy's hand. She knew it belonged to Ferox, the nine-year-old in charge of the younger cutpurses. He must have been looking for her all this time.

Bouda hated Ferox and considered biting his hand, but his

reaction might cause the soldiers, who were already moving away, to come back, so she let herself go limp instead.

After the two legionaries had disappeared into the fog, Ferox dragged her out from under the wagon. 'Where were you? Did you get any purses?'

When Bouda refused to answer he reached down the front of her belted tunic and found two money pouches. She had cut their strings with the small folding knife tied around her wrist.

Smirking, he took the pouches, and when she glared at him he pinched her bare arms to make her squeal. But Bouda refused to make a sound. Even when he slapped her face she remained stubbornly silent.

With a muttered oath Ferox grabbed her wrist and dragged her back along the foggy wharf, between crates, amphoras and barrels and finally up dark wooden stairs to the upper floor of a warehouse. Tyranus sat behind a table laden with items from the morning's haul. He was examining the carving in a signet ring.

'Bouda nearly got caught by two Roman soldiers,' said Ferox, still gripping her arm so hard that it hurt. 'They think she's Boudica's great-granddaughter. They were talking about sending her to Rome to be in the Emperor's triumphal procession.'

The boss of the East End Gang got up, came round the table and squatted down so that his head was level with Bouda's. Tyranus had large dark eyes with long eyelashes and would have been good-looking, if not for the scar across his nose. 'You know what Domitian does to little girls?' he said in a voice as soft as velvet. 'He does horrible things. And then he eats them.'

Bouda stared bravely back at him, her mouth clamped shut. She was determined not to cry.

Tyranus stood up and shook his head. He glanced at Ferox. 'Did she at least cut a purse or two?'

'No,' Ferox lied. He released his grip on Bouda and pulled out three pouches. They included the two he had found down the front of her tunic. 'I got these, but she's useless.' He spat on Bouda's bare foot. She managed not to flinch.

'Don't be so hard on the girl,' said Tyranus, emptying the contents of the purses on to the table. 'She is only six. Still . . .' He picked up a thin rod made of birch and turned to Bouda. 'You know the rules,' he said. 'If you come back empty-handed, you get the rod.'

Bouda nodded, shot Ferox a glare and then grinned. She brought her right hand to her mouth and spat out the pearl she had been holding in her cheek for nearly an hour.

It was covered with saliva but that only made it gleam more.

'Well, well, well.' Tyranus put down the rod and took the pearl. 'Look at that. The best tribute I've had all week. You did well, my little flame.' He patted Bouda's head. 'Tonight you'll get a slice of bread and honey as your reward, and you can sleep nearest the brazier.'

Ferox gave her a filthy look as she followed him out, but Bouda didn't care. She felt her heart swell with happiness. Tyranus was proud of her!

'Remember, Bouda,' Tyranus called after them. 'Gold and gems and pearls are the only things that will keep you safe in this world.'

Later that night, huddled on the sleeping mat with the other girls, Bouda was content. What made her happy was not the bread and honey in her stomach or her place nearest the brazier, but the memory of Tyranus's look of pride and his words of praise. They warmed her more than any coals in a bronze tripod.

'Gold and gems and pearls,' she whispered, 'are the only things that will keep me safe in this world.'

Chapter One
GLADIATRIX

Seven years later, Bouda wasn't running from Romans; she was fighting them.

Or rather, she was fighting one: a fourteen-year-old boy called Lucius Domitius Juba.

The combat was not taking place in Londinium's great amphitheatre, but in the inner courtyard of a Roman-style villa on the outskirts of a town called Verulamium.

Bouda was armed with a sword and a semi-circular shield called a pelta. Instead of a helmet she had plaited her hair into two dozen beaded braids that caressed her shoulders like Medusa's snaky locks. And instead of heavy armour she wore a leather breast band and a short tartan kilt in orange and green wool.

She knew her beauty was one of her best weapons.

But a blade was useful too.

'Aieeee!' Bouda gave the Iceni war cry as she swept her sword towards her opponent's neck.

'Ungh!' Juba grunted as he dodged the swipe. He was dressed as a retiarius, with padded legs and arms, a trident in his left hand and a net in his right.

In a fluid dancer's move, Bouda twirled and brought her

sword down from the other side. This time Juba managed to block the sword with his trident, but one of the outer prongs shattered under the force of her blow.

Bouda laughed at the expression on his face.

It was only a mock battle fought with wooden weapons, but she was not holding back.

A year and a half before, she had noticed brown-skinned Juba getting off a boat in Londinium with his brother and sister. The three of them were obviously rich and clueless. Seeing her chance for a better life, Bouda had offered her services as a guide. Not long after, a Roman woman named Flavia Gemina recruited the four of them to become unofficial Questers of lost children.

In the past year and a half they had returned over a dozen kidnapped children to their parents, reunited twins separated in infancy and even tracked down an adult friend of Flavia's, a young doctor named Jonathan ben Mordecai.

They had also quelled a possible Druid uprising.

Most of their work had been behind the scenes, but after a spectacularly public rescue at a town named Camulodunum, they retreated to the safety of this villa outside Verulamium. The secluded Roman-style house was owned by one of Flavia's freedmen, a Briton who had become rich and returned to the province of his birth.

Bouda and her friends had spent the long winter months studying philosophy in the mornings, practising combat skills in the afternoons and hiding whenever someone came from town to make a delivery.

On this day, Bouda's mock battle with Juba was entertainment at a farewell banquet for the twin boys they had helped reunite. Castor and his brother Raven were departing for Rome the following day.

As Bouda and Juba circled each other, she saw him wipe away a trickle of sweat. This was surprising because it was a chilly spring morning and he was practically naked. He wore only a gladiator's loincloth plus the cotton padding on his shins and left arm. She reckoned he was sweating with nervousness because of the three surprise guests at the banquet.

Their patroness Flavia Gemina, her husband and the governor himself had unexpectedly joined the celebration.

'Aieeee!' Bouda yelled again as she swung her sword down in another strong arc. This blow shattered the other outer prong of his trident. Juba stared open-mouthed at her. In all their months of drilling none of them had used enough force to break one of their practice weapons. Now she had left him with a strange-looking spear.

She laughed and slashed at his belly. He leapt back, barely avoiding a nasty scratch, for even a wooden practice sword could do damage. Once again they circled each other, and Bouda could hear what the diners were saying.

'Who is the lovely red-haired girl?' asked the governor, reclining in the place of honour. 'Is she also one of your so-called Questers?'

'Yes,' came Flavia's reply. 'Isn't she good? Because my Questers are often in danger I thought they should learn some combat skills before their next mission. So Bouda and Juba's sister Ursula have both been training with the boys. The owner of this house is a former gladiator. He's been teaching them.'

'Fascinating,' said the governor. 'With her fiery hair, the girl reminds me of that barbarian queen who almost sent us packing thirty-five years ago.'

'Boudica!' said Flavia's husband.

At the mention of her great-grandmother, Bouda's

11

concentration slipped for a moment, allowing Juba to knock her sideways with the shaft of his broken trident.

Instead of resisting the blow she went with it, rolling and then leaping lightly to her feet. It had not hurt, and she realised Juba was holding back. The knowledge gave her strength.

'Watch out, philosopher boy!' She tossed her plaited hair. 'If you're Aeneas, then I'm Camilla!' She feinted one way, then lunged the other. But he wasn't fooled. His net caught her pelta and after a moment's struggle she let the shield go.

'Aeneas and Camilla never faced each other,' he growled, tossing aside the net-entangled pelta.

'But if they had,' said Bouda, 'then this might have happened!' She somersaulted forward and jabbed her sword at his lean brown torso. Juba twisted his body away, then cursed as the sword slid along his ribcage.

'Ha!' cried Bouda. 'If my sword had been metal and not wooden, your entrails would be spilling out onto the dirt!'

Juba grunted as he thrust the remaining cork-tipped prong of his wooden trident at her, then swung its shaft at the back of her knees to bring her down.

But she could tell his heart wasn't in it; he missed both times. She heard him curse under his breath.

'Don't let pity rule you!' cried Prasutus, a young Briton who had been hiding out with them all winter. He had once dabbled in Druid arts but had now joined them to study the teachings of Epicurus, Seneca and Jesus. 'A good Stoic is always in control!'

'Come on, Juba!' yelled Juba's younger sister Ursula from the couch beside Prasutus. '*Carpe diem!* Seize the moment!'

'*Carpe diem!*' echoed Loquax the mynah bird from his perch on Ursula's shoulder. '*Carpe diem!*'

Juba grinned at this encouragement, but Bouda scowled.

She hated it when the others ganged up against her. Grabbing a handful of sandy dirt from the herb bed that ringed their practice area, she made a tossing gesture at the bird. Loquax fluttered up in alarm.

But she had only pretended to fling the dirt.

A moment later she tossed it into Juba's face instead.

While he was still spitting and blinking, she hurled herself at him. A moment later she had him flat on his back. Her knees pinned his arms to the ground and her wooden sword pressed the side of his throat.

Bouda heard the twins laugh, but Flavia Gemina gasped and the governor exclaimed in protest.

'Unfair!' he spluttered. 'Is that the sort of move your freedman has been teaching them?'

Flavia Gemina sounded apologetic. 'He would never teach them such a thing. Perhaps she learned it on the streets of Londinium in her days as a cutpurse.'

Bouda ignored them and grinned down at Juba. She noticed the black pupils of his grey-green eyes were bigger than usual. She leaned down. 'Prasutus is wrong,' she whispered. 'You have too much control. You should let your passions loose!'

She leaned closer, letting her snake-like plaits tickle his ears. The priceless gem around her neck dangled, too, and that gave her an idea.

'The most important Roman in the province is watching,' she said into his ear. 'I know you value honour above all else. Promise to give me one of the jewels sewn into the seam of your cloak. Then I'll let you win.'

As soon as she saw the look on his face, she knew she had said the wrong thing.

Chapter Two
PATRONA

Juba stared up at Bouda's beautiful face.

From the day she had approached them with her sly green eyes, brazen hair and promise of help, he had not trusted her motives. She had been raised to value only riches and was a thief at heart. It had taken a year and a half for him to believe that she was learning to value friendship more than riches.

So when she offered to let him win in exchange for a gem, bitter disappointment flooded his heart.

'You'll *let* me win?' he hissed. 'Why, you greedy little vixen!'

So far he had been holding back, but now he bucked his whole body and a moment later their positions were reversed. Now he was on top and pressing her own wooden sword against her slim white neck.

'Ha!' came the governor's voice. 'I knew the boy was holding back! Where did you say he comes from? Syria, perhaps?'

Flavia Gemina laughed. 'Don't let his brown skin fool you. He's as Roman as you or I. You met him last year, remember?'

She didn't tell the governor that Juba and his siblings had once lived a stone's throw from the Emperor's palace in Rome and that they were now wanted for treason and theft. As far

14

as the governor knew, Juba was just another one of the stray children she tried to help.

'Come on, Roman boy!' called the governor. 'Vanquish the Briton girl!'

Juba glowered down at Bouda. 'Do you submit?'

She writhed beneath him and violently shook her head. The amusement in her eyes had been replaced with genuine panic. When he saw her terror, Juba's anger faded. But before he could let her go, something pricked his left wrist. Juba looked down in astonishment to see blood spurting from a nick in his flesh.

'What the . . .?'

He looked from his bloody wrist to the bright object in her right hand.

It was the small folding knife she always wore, left over from her days as a cutpurse.

'You cut me!' He got off her and stood up, staring at the blood oozing from his wound. 'I can't believe you actually cut me.'

'Pause!' called the referee who was also their trainer and the owner of the house.

'I'm sorry, Juba!' Bouda scrambled to her feet. 'I felt trapped and it just happened!'

She seemed genuinely upset so he shrugged. 'Don't worry,' he said, sucking the wound. 'We'll call it a draw.'

'No we won't!' Their trainer came forward. He was wearing a tan and blue tartan tunic over dark blue leggings. 'The throwing of dirt and use of unauthorised weapons disqualifies you, Bouda.'

He quickly wrapped a strip of linen around Juba's left wrist and tied it off. Then he held up Juba's right arm. 'I declare Juba the winner!'

Everyone cheered and the governor pronounced, 'Roman honour conquers the crafty barbarian!'

As the trainer dropped Juba's arm and stepped back, Bouda scowled at Juba. 'If this had been a real combat,' she muttered, 'you would be dead and I would have won. Remember that!'

Juba glared back at her. 'Why don't you ever play fair?' he said through gritted teeth.

Her green eyes almost sent off sparks. 'Play fair? Like your hero, pious Aeneas? You think you're pious, too, don't you? But you ran away from Rome like a coward. Then you sold your baby sister to pay for your passage to Britannia. You're not pious; you're a coward!'

Juba slapped her.

Hard.

Her eyes opened wide, and so did her mouth. A red mark appeared on her pale cheek. Horrified, he saw that it was in the shape of a handprint.

His handprint.

'Bouda!' he gasped. 'Bouda, I'm sorry!'

But she had already turned her back on him and was stalking out of the courtyard.

'*What ARE you doing?*' cried Loquax the talking bird. It was one of his favourite expressions.

'Pollux!' cursed Flavia's husband. 'That's not good.'

The governor had been reclining but now he was sitting upright. 'You sold your baby sister?' he asked Juba. 'A freeborn girl?'

'He had no choice!' cried Ursula from the couch next to his. 'We were being chased by the Praetorian Guard!' Then she clapped her hands over her mouth.

'What?' The governor was on his feet. '*WHAT?*'

Juba cursed under his breath. The governor was not supposed to know they were enemies of the Emperor. And now Bouda and his sister had put them in an impossible situation.

The governor was looking at Flavia Gemina and her husband in disbelief. 'You've been sponsoring enemies of the Emperor while under my protection?'

Flavia's husband slid off the couch. 'Sir, I'm sorry. I promise you; I had no idea. You know how headstrong my wife can be.'

The governor's fists were clenched. 'Do you know what Domitian does to those who show even the least whiff of betrayal?'

At this mention of the Emperor's name, Ursula's talking bird chimed in. '*Cave Domitian!*' cried Loquax. '*Beware of Domitian!*'

'Dear Jupiter!' cried the governor, his usually florid face as pale as chalk. 'You've even trained your bird to be a traitor. We're all doomed!' He summoned his slave-boy to put on his boots. A moment later he rushed out of the courtyard, followed by the boy.

'Sir, wait!' Flavia's husband slid off the couch, pulled on his own shoes and then hurried after his patron.

'*Eheu!* Alas!' cried Flavia. Her face was pale as she looked after the governor and her husband. Then she ran to the twins, who were sitting side by side on the edge of their couch. 'Farewell, dear cousins!' She gave each of them a hasty kiss. 'In case I don't see you before you go, may the gods carry you safely back home.'

'*Cave Domitian!*' said Loquax in his eerily human-sounding voice. '*Cave Domitian!*'

Juba had taken off his protective padding and was pulling on his faded green tunic. 'Ursula!' he cried as his head emerged. 'For the sake of all the gods, silence that bird!' Then he looked at his patroness. 'I'm so sorry, domina. What can we do to make this better?'

'Don't worry!' Flavia Gemina was backing out of the courtyard and making a patting motion with both hands. 'I'll try to smooth things over with the governor. But for Juno's sake, stay inside and out of sight or you'll get us all arrested and executed!'

Chapter Three
OSCILLUM

Ursula felt terrible. By blurting out their secret she had put their lives in danger.

She scrambled off her couch and called after Flavia Gemina. 'Domina, I'm so sorry!' But their patroness did not look back.

'*Cave Domitian!*' said Loquax cheerfully. '*Beware of Domitian!*'

'Ursula!' Juba stalked over to her. 'Silence your bird!'

In an instant, Ursula's enormous dog Gartha was out from under the dining couches and growling at Juba.

Gartha wasn't Ursula's only defender. Prasutus took a stand on her other side. 'Don't be so hard on her! It's not her fault.'

'Yes it is!' Juba closed his eyes and took a deep breath. 'Haven't you heard what we've been talking about for the last few weeks?' he said to Ursula. 'About all the terrible things Domitian has been doing? He just executed his own cousin, for Jupiter's sake! What do you think he would do if he found we'd trained a bird to say *Beware Domitian?*'

Ursula fought back tears. 'We've been stuck here for nearly nine months! I just wanted to see if I could teach Loquax something new. I didn't think anyone would hear us!'

Prasutus nodded. 'We're beginning to peck at each other like chickens cooped up too long.'

'Then sail with us tomorrow!' offered Raven. He was one of the twins they had reunited, a startlingly handsome youth with grey eyes and silky black hair.

'Yes!' said his identical twin brother Castor. 'My grandmother has a beautiful villa just outside Rome's port of Ostia, by the synagogue. There are lots of rooms there. Enough for all of us.'

'Ostia is too close to Rome,' said Juba. 'That would be like going into the lion's den. Thank you for the offer, but we can't put you in danger. It's bad enough that we've put our host at risk,' he added. 'He's been incredibly generous with food and drink and wood for hot water.'

'I know.' Ursula stared miserably at the mosaic floor of the triclinium. Then she took a deep breath. 'I suppose now is not a good time to tell you that Loquax probably used to be Domitian's pet . . .'

'What?' Juba yelped. 'You stole the Emperor's pet?'

Once again Gartha growled at him.

Ursula silenced the growl with a reassuring pat on Gartha's head. 'You know I didn't steal him!' she said. 'He flew into an oscillum. Remember?'

'What's an oscillum?' asked Prasutus.

'It's a marble disc. You hang them between the columns of a courtyard. They have scary masks painted on them and revolve slowly. They're supposed to keep away evil.'

'And birds,' said Juba.

'Only it didn't work for Loquax.' Ursula looked affectionately at the black and yellow bird on her shoulder. 'You flew into one and broke your wing, didn't you?'

'*Cave Domitian!*' said Loquax happily.

'And you would have died if I hadn't nursed you back to health.'

'Dear gods,' cried Juba. 'Why didn't we see it before? An exotic talking bird trained to say *Ave, Domitian!* And the Emperor's palace was only a stone's throw from our villa. Of course the bird was the Emperor's!'

'That was almost four years ago,' Ursula pointed out. 'When Loquax first arrived, I mean. We were only little.'

'I was eleven,' said Juba. 'I should have realised.'

'Pater and Mater should have realised,' said Ursula.

For a moment they were both silent, remembering the parents who had sacrificed their lives to give them time to escape. Ursula had never seen their bodies, but Juba had. They had drunk hemlock so the Emperor's torturers couldn't make them tell where they had hidden all their wealth or where their children had gone.

Juba turned to Ursula. 'When did you first realise that Loquax was Domitian's pet?'

Ursula glanced at Prasutus, who gave a little nod.

'Last year,' she admitted. 'At Camulodunum, when Prasutus and I were taken to the legate's house with that fat man named Montanus. Loquax came with us. The legate said the Emperor used to have a talking bird trained to greet him.'

Juba frowned. 'Was Montanus there at the time?'

Ursula nodded. 'He said the Emperor's talking bird was worth as much as an educated Greek slave.'

'Great Jupiter's eyebrows!' cried Juba. 'Montanus was one of the Emperor's closest friends. And he went back to Rome nine months ago! What if he told Domitian that a brown-skinned girl has his precious talking bird? Domitian will know we're in Britannia.'

'He already knows! That's why we've been hiding out here all winter!'

'He was never certain. His guards might have seen us board a ship bound for Britannia but they couldn't be sure that we arrived safely or that we are even still alive. But if Montanus told him about you and the talking bird, then Domitian will know for sure where we are.'

'He might know we're in Britannia, but he wouldn't know we're staying in a villa near the town of Verulamium . . .'

Juba frowned as he paced back and forth. 'No, but now that the governor knows, he'll have to report us . . .'

'That's why you should leave this place and come with us,' said Raven.

'At least sail with us part way,' said Castor. 'We can drop you at any port.'

'But Flavia Gemina told us to wait here and not go anywhere,' said Juba.

'Shhhh!' Prasutus was holding up his hand. 'Is someone knocking at the door?'

They were all silent. Then Ursula nodded. Someone was banging on the double doors at the front of the house. Had the governor returned? Or Flavia and her husband?

The owner of the house came into the garden, a grim expression on his face. 'Soldiers at the door,' he said to Juba and Ursula. 'They asked for you by name.'

Ursula stared at the others in dismay.

The governor had obviously decided to arrest them.

And it was all her fault.

Chapter Four
NUNTIUS

When Juba hurried into the atrium and saw the two soldiers framed in the wide-open doorway, he breathed a sigh of relief.

It was his older brother, Fronto, and his friend Vindex, who had been serving as part of the governor's troops in Londinium. They belonged to a cohort of auxiliary archers and were carrying their bows and arrows. Both wore long tunics under brass fish-scale armour. Their oval shields bore the sign of the Syrian Scorpions: a red scorpion on yellow. The white ostrich-feather plumes atop their conical helmets fluttered in the chill spring breeze.

'Fronto!' cried Juba. 'Don't tell me you've come to arrest us?'

'Of course not!' Fronto made no move to enter, but remained outside. 'Why would you think that?'

'Because you're part of the governor's bodyguard and the governor was just here. Didn't you see him?'

'No,' said Fronto. 'Probably because we stopped at a temple in Verulamium to ask the gods for a favourable outcome.'

'And then we had to ask directions,' said Vindex. 'We didn't know you were staying a few miles outside the town.'

'It's better being outside the town,' said Juba. 'Very few people come here. And if we don't want to be seen, we can just go into the inner courtyard.'

'May we come in?' said Fronto.

'Of course!' cried Juba.

Fronto touched the door frame, right, left, right, before stepping over the threshold with his right foot. Then he put down his shield and weapons so that he could embrace his brother as much as the scale armour would allow.

'We didn't mean to frighten you,' he said to Juba. 'We assumed your door slave knew who we were!' He gestured at the big Briton in a long checked tunic of pale blue and fawn over dark blue leggings.

Juba grinned and shook his head. 'Caudex isn't the door slave,' he said. 'He's the owner of this house. He's a freedman of Flavia Gemina. He and his wife have been hosting us all winter. And Caudex has been teaching us gladiator skills.'

'Apologies, sir,' said Fronto politely and inclined his head. Vindex nodded too.

'You are most welcome,' said Caudex. 'Come into the inner courtyard and take refreshment.'

'Is it safe?' Ursula's head peeped out from a column, along with Prasutus's head and the twins'. Then she squealed, 'Fronto!' and ran into the atrium. The others all came in after her and greeted Fronto and Vindex.

Bouda was the last to come in. She had put on her clothes and undone her plaits so that her copper hair flowed loose in wavy kinks. Juba noticed that Caudex's little girl, Fortunata, was clinging to the skirt of her tartan tunic.

As Bouda went up to Fronto, the sun emerged from a cloud and shone through the skylight above the rainwater pool. It made her hair glow almost as much as his brass fish-scale armour. The two of them were radiant as they stood facing each other.

'Bouda!' said Fronto. 'You've grown!'

'You've grown, too!' She smiled. 'And your voice is deeper!'

Juba felt a flash of jealousy as Bouda gave Fronto a kiss on the cheek. His brother was taller and more muscular than the last time he had seen him.

'My voice is deeper, too!' Vindex raised his hand.

'And we both have to visit the barber,' said Fronto.

'At least twice a week.' Vindex grinned and gave his chin a rub.

Bouda gave Vindex a kiss on the cheek too. 'I can almost feel your beard,' she said with a laugh and then stepped back awkwardly on account of the little girl still clinging to her stola.

'What brings you here?' Juba asked his brother.

Fronto took a deep breath. 'Some of our cohort is going abroad. To Colonia Claudia Ara Agrippinensium.'

'Where?' said Bouda and Juba together.

'It's the capital city of Germania Inferior. We're going to be special agents for the governor of that province.'

'Will it be dangerous?' asked Ursula.

Fronto made the sign against evil. 'No,' he said. 'If the gods are willing, it won't be dangerous. But our commander will be a man called Trajan. Does that name mean anything to you?' he asked Juba.

Juba frowned. 'No, I don't think so.'

'Do you remember about six years ago?' said Fronto. 'When you were eight and I was ten, and Pater took us to see the procession celebrating Domitian's triumph over the rebel Saturninus?'

Juba frowned. 'Was that the parade with decaying human

25

heads stuck on spears?' He shuddered. 'It gave me nightmares for ages.'

'Who was Saturninus?' asked Bouda.

'He was a Roman officer stationed in Germania,' said Fronto. 'He convinced two legions to join him in a rebellion against Domitian. He might have succeeded if the river hadn't thawed and kept his German reinforcements from reaching him.'

Castor snapped his fingers. 'Trajan was one of the commanders who marched against Saturninus,' he said.

Fronto looked impressed. 'That's right,' he said. 'Trajan and his legion hurried all the way from Spain. They made record time, but by the time they got there Saturninus had been defeated. Although Trajan arrived too late to help, Domitian rewarded his loyalty by giving him command of several legions in that region. Guess where he spends most of his time?'

'Colonia Claudia Ara Agrippinensium?' asked Castor.

'Exactly.'

Juba raised both eyebrows. 'So you're going to be serving under one of Domitian's most loyal commanders?'

Fronto nodded. 'Still, we'll be out and about a lot. Also, I'm with the Syrians and using my false name. Hopefully he won't link me to the warrant for our arrest. But who knows what the gods have in store for any of us? That's why I wanted to come to say farewell. And also . . .' His voice trailed off.

Juba noticed he was tapping the hem of his fish-scale tunic, right, left, right. It was something he had done when he was younger, whenever he was afraid or nervous.

'Fronto?' Juba asked. 'Is everything all right?'

Fronto nodded and glanced at Bouda. 'It's just that a few of the men are bringing their wives.'

'Wives?' Juba felt queasy about the direction the conversation was taking. 'But soldiers aren't allowed to marry.'

'True. But our cohort commander is Syrian. He's not as strict as some of the Roman officers. He allows women to travel with the baggage carts and live in the settlements by the forts. There are still four places on board the ship taking us across the channel. Soldiers aren't officially allowed to marry but our commander has said we can bring wives anyway.'

As Fronto turned to Bouda, Juba's heart began to thud. He knew his older brother loved Bouda but he could not believe this was happening.

'Bouda,' said Fronto, 'I have something to ask you.'

Everyone was looking at Bouda, even little Fortunata.

Juba turned to her too. Her face was pale and her eyes wide.

He knew what she was thinking. Fronto loved her. Since the first day in Londinium when she had taken his hand and asked him to help her, his adoration had been obvious. At least until last year, when he met Bircha, a lovely girl of the Atrebates tribe who had been training to be a Druid priestess.

But it seemed that Fronto had forgotten Bircha. He was looking at Bouda with something like awe in his eyes.

Juba's stomach suddenly felt as small and hard as a walnut.

In that moment he saw three versions of Bouda, just as he could sometimes detect traces of previous notes on a wax tablet.

He saw thirteen-year-old Bouda, standing before him now in the bloom of her first beauty.

He saw the frightened little thief Bouda had once been.

And he also saw the brave, wise woman she could become.

Juba could not imagine a life without all three Boudas in it.

Was his older brother about to take her away from him?

Chapter Five
NUPTIAE

The next day, Juba felt a pang of envy as Fronto entered the sunny courtyard with his bride-to-be. The emotion annoyed him. A Stoic should not allow himself such petty feelings.

And why was he envious anyway?

He should be feeling relieved that Fronto's request to Bouda had been not for her hand in marriage, but for the lucky nettle-cloth undertunic she had been weaving for over half a year. Fronto was obsessed with lucky objects and this was to be a gift for his bride, the beautiful British girl named Bircha.

Perhaps he was envious because Fronto's bride was so beautiful. With her willowy body, blue eyes and hair the colour of moonlight, Bircha was even lovelier than Bouda.

But Juba preferred Bouda's temperament. Bouda was bold where Bircha was shy. Bouda was complicated, but Bircha was as pure and innocent as water in a mountain brook. Bouda's face hid her thoughts, but Bircha's revealed every emotion. Even through the gauzy orange veil, Juba could see the look of love in Bircha's eyes.

Fronto was also incapable of hiding his feelings, and it was clear that he and Bircha adored each other.

Maybe that was what Juba envied: the total commitment each had for the other.

Juba gave Bouda a sidelong glance. She stood beside him at the edge of the garden courtyard, dressed in her best blue cape with its soft beaver-skin collar over a tunic of fine wool in squares of green, blue, cream and orange. Her copper hair was done up in a soft twist with dangling tendrils. She was watching the couple with hooded eyes and he could see she had smudged her eyelids with something smoky to make them look more mysterious.

Did she love Fronto?

Had she been disappointed when he asked for a tunic rather than her hand in marriage?

Juba rubbed his left wrist where Bouda had cut it the day before. He didn't mind that she had cut him. She only lashed out when she was frightened or scared. That was the little Bouda. The one he longed to comfort.

A tug on the left-hand side of his cloak brought Juba's attention to his sister, Ursula.

'Pay attention!' she hissed. 'This is an important day for Fronto!'

Juba turned his eyes back to his brother, who was looking at him expectantly.

'The ring!' hissed Bouda on his right. 'Give him the ring.'

With a muttered oath, Juba fished in his belt pouch and brought out the ring. A simple gold setting held one of the gems his mother had sewn into the seam of his father's cloak a year and a half ago, shortly before they had fled Rome. The small oval aquamarine bore a carving of a tiny cupid stringing a bow. The image spoke of love and archery, and the colour matched Bircha's eyes perfectly.

Two strides brought Juba to Fronto's side. As he placed the ring in the palm of his brother's hand, he felt it trembling. Fronto was nervous!

Juba smiled encouragingly and patted his brother's shoulder, then stepped back.

Fronto slipped the ring on the fourth finger of Bircha's left hand. Then, as they clasped right hands for all to see, he said, 'I promise to provide for you and to protect you.'

Bircha spoke the ancient response: '*Ubi tu Gaius, ibi ego Gaia*. Where you are Gaius, there will I be Gaia.'

With these two phrases, and the clasping of right hands, the ceremony was over. Bircha pulled back her saffron-coloured veil and kissed him.

Everyone cheered and some of the guests tossed beans and raisins at them. The beans would keep away bad luck and the raisins would ensure many sons and daughters. Bircha laughed and covered them both with the protective tent of her veil. Juba saw them kissing again under the filmy yellow fabric.

Then a pantomime troupe struck up a jaunty wedding song in their honour. The famous pantomime dancer Lupus and his wife, Clio, had recently taken on Bircha and her brother, Bolianus, as musicians. They would be sailing with the Syrians the following day, as they had never toured Belgica or Germania before.

Juba sidestepped closer to Bouda. 'I hope you're not too disappointed,' he said in a low voice.

'Why would I be disappointed?'

'Because you love Fronto?'

'What makes you think that?'

'You spent months weaving that nettle-cloth tunic for him.'

Bouda arched a dark eyebrow and turned her head to whisper in his ear. 'Because I knew he would appreciate it.'

Juba stared at her.

'So you don't love him?'

The others had all joined in with the wedding song, even little Fortunata. Bouda shook her head. 'I like Fronto. But I never loved him.'

'But I thought . . . When you were at the sanctuary of Aquae Sulis, Ursula overheard you asking the goddess to protect the boy you loved.'

Bouda brought her lips so close to his ear that he could feel her breath. 'I *did* ask the goddess to protect the boy I loved. But I wasn't talking about Fronto.'

Juba felt his cheeks grow hot. Did Bouda mean him?

He was grateful that his dusky skin hid all but the most violent blushes.

Then he remembered there were two much more likely candidates for her affection. 'Castor?' he said. 'Is it Castor you love? Or Raven?'

They both looked across the garden at the pair of identically handsome boys who had just joined in the song. The twins had delayed their departure by a day in order to take part in the festivities. At fifteen, Castor and Raven were at the peak of their beauty. With their jet-black hair, full lips and skin as smooth and pale as marble, they were prettier than most girls.

'No,' said Bouda, 'I don't love either of them. They're too unpredictable. I need someone steadier to anchor me.'

Juba's face flooded with warmth. Again.

He remembered a festival in a British grove with a feast and a bonfire. Bouda had taken his hand and danced with him. At the time, he assumed she was trying to cheer him up after the theft of his clothes in the bathhouse at Aquae Sulis. Had it been something more?

Bouda had spent hours in his classes when he had been teaching the villagers to read, write and declaim Latin. And in the past nine months she had been coming to the classes he taught on rhetoric, philosophy and epic poetry. Of Raven, Castor, Prasutus and Ursula, she was his most devoted pupil.

Suddenly his heart was going like a drum.

He loved Bouda and she loved him.

How had he never seen it before?

Was she too young to marry? In Rome a girl had to be at least twelve years old.

He was almost certain she was thirteen.

'Bouda?'

'Yes?' She was giving him her amused look. But he wasn't going to let that put him off.

'Are you of marriageable age?'

'What?'

'I mean, how old are you? When were you born?'

'I don't know exactly.' She twirled a strand of copper hair around her finger. 'Tyranus used to say one of his girls found me in a basket among the tombs outside Londinium about this time of year. Around the Ides of April. He thinks I was between four and five months old.'

Juba was about to ask how many years ago that had been when the image of his own baby sister, Dora, rose up before him. She had been five months old when he traded her for their passage to Britannia. He looked at Caudex's little girl, Fortunata, who was holding a cat in her chubby arms and trying to dance with her. His little sister Dora would now be Fortunata's age.

Assuming she was still alive.

How could he think of moving on with his own life until he had put that right? His mother's dying words to him had been '*Save the children*' and he had failed.

'Did you hear me, Juba?' Bouda's voice seemed to come from a great distance. 'I think I'm at least thirteen. You're fourteen, aren't you? Almost a man.'

He nodded absently. 'I'm almost old enough to put on the toga virilis, the manly tunic,' he murmured. He turned away so Bouda would not see the anguish on his face. And to himself he muttered, 'Some man! I can't even look after my own family.'

Chapter Six
NOX

A crack of thunder woke Bouda some time after midnight. It was three days after Fronto's wedding and, although it was April, winter had returned with steady rain and a chilly wind.

And now a storm.

The sleeping cubicle she shared with Ursula was briefly lit by a faint flash of silver. Bouda waited for the thunder.

When the long deep rumble finally came, it seemed like a warning.

It had been four days since the governor had discovered her friends' secret: that they were wanted by the Emperor. Flavia Gemina had told them to lie low and wait for instructions. But four days felt like too long. What if soldiers were already on their way to arrest Juba and Ursula?

A few days ago she thought Juba was about to tell her he cared for her. Maybe even ask her to marry him. But he hadn't. Even after she had practically confessed her feelings for him.

The thought of that rejection brought tears to her eyes. He would never care for her the way she cared for him. She had been trying so hard to learn the Stoic philosophy and live a virtuous life but even after all this time he didn't trust her. She often saw it in his eyes when he didn't think she was watching. That thought made her angry, so she blinked back the tears and hardened her heart.

She had stayed with Juba and his sister for a year and a half. It wasn't as if she owed them anything. Quite the opposite, in fact. They owed her. Surely she deserved some reward for all the help she had given them?

Bouda touched the Minerva gem around her neck. Juba had given it to her a year before so that she could have a special goddess to pray to as he and his siblings did.

Carved of a single piece of sardonyx in several different colours, it showed the goddess Minerva in profile with a helmet, and a tiny Medusa on her breastplate. On account of its superb craftsmanship, and because it had once belonged to the Emperor Augustus, it was worth a fortune, enough to buy a house or a ship.

Bouda's mind raced. If she crept out now she could easily make her way to Londinium, go to a man she knew who bought stolen goods and get a good price for the Minerva gem. Then she could buy a passage to anywhere in the Empire and still have money left over to buy a small townhouse or farm. She would never have to rely on anyone again.

A strange wheezy noise was coming from Ursula's bed. Years ago, someone had cut Gartha's vocal chords so she could not bark. But she could still whine and she was doing so now.

Bouda lifted herself up on one elbow. Ursula snored softly, but Gartha was definitely whining.

Bouda pushed back her blanket, got out of bed and pulled on her felt slippers. When she went to the door of their small room she could see part of the main garden courtyard, dimly lit by a single flickering wall torch. Was something out there?

Gartha came up beside her, a warm furry bulk in the darkness.

Bouda patted Gartha for courage, took a breath and stepped out into the dark colonnade. A gust of wind brought the strong smell of rain. Aware of Gartha padding behind, she made her way to the central garden. As she reached the triclinium, a flash of lightning showed a cloaked figure with his back to her.

Bouda gasped and made the sign against evil.

The figure turned and said, 'Bouda?'

'Oh, Juba!' She breathed a sigh of relief.

He was wearing his father's birrus Britannicus with the hood up against the gusting wind and rain.

'Are you all right?' He took a step towards her, coming so close that she could feel the warmth of his body.

She nodded and shivered. 'The thunder woke me,' she said. 'What if it's a bad omen? What if Castor and Raven's ship has been sunk? Or Fronto's? What if the Emperor's men are finally coming to get you?'

'Don't worry,' he said. And his voice was so full of compassion that she felt her heart soften like a honeycomb in the sun.

She stifled a sob. Maybe he did care for her.

And she had been thinking of running away.

'Oh, Bouda! Don't cry.'

He put his arms around her.

Bouda stiffened.

She was not used to people touching her. But after a moment she let herself relax against him and allowed the tears come.

His arms were around her and he was rocking slightly. Nobody had ever held her quite like this before. She had grown up in a gang of children. The only human contact she had known was at night when she and the other girls huddled together on the sleeping mat for warmth.

The smell of him was comforting: a slight muskiness overlaid with damp wool. She breathed him in and let the sobs shake her body. The arms encircling her felt skinnier but also stronger than she had imagined. She felt safer than she had in years.

'I'm sorry, Juba.' Her voice was muffled by his cloak. 'I'm sorry I cut you and called you a coward the other day. And I'm sorry I tried to make you give me a jewel. After all, I already have the Minerva gem.'

Juba let go of her and stepped back. Away from the warmth of his body and the feel of his arms, she felt abandoned.

'That was only a loan. So you could have a god to pray to, like the rest of us. I have Mercury, Fronto has Jupiter Ammon and Ursula had that little ivory Venus.'

'Of course,' she said. But she felt something tighten around her heart, as if he had tied a ribbon around it. 'It's just that I thought you might let me keep it.'

'You do know that it is worth a fortune, don't you?'

Bouda felt the ribbon of fear tighten and start to choke her. So she turned the fear into anger. 'So what? You don't need it! You've already got a fortune in gems sewn into the seams of your cloak!'

'I only have a few jewels left!' he muttered. 'The Minerva gem is worth more than all of them put together. And it belonged to my mother. It was her parting gift to me.'

'She gave it to you so you could sell it and buy your passage to Britannia.'

'And it was stolen.'

'But you got it back,' she hissed, 'partly thanks to me!'

37

'It's still mine!' A flash of lightning lit his face and she saw the anger in his eyes.

Gartha growled at Juba and he glared down at the big dog. 'I'm not going to hurt her,' he said between clenched teeth. 'I'm just making sure she knows what's hers and what is not.'

A moment before, Bouda had felt safe and accepted in his embrace. Now he was telling her the Minerva gem was not hers to keep.

That gem was her security, her bedrock, her foundation.

Before Juba could ask her to return the priceless gem, she turned and stumbled back towards her dark bedroom.

Gold and gems and pearls, said Tyranus's voice in her head, *are the only things that will keep you safe in this world.*

She had put her trust in people, not treasure. That was her mistake.

Juba didn't trust her. He still thought she was a thief and a liar.

So be it.

She waited for at least an hour before putting on her spare tunic, her fur-collared cloak and her boots.

Then, clutching the Minerva gem for courage, she crept through the stormy colonnades of the villa to the double front doors. There she hesitated, her heart thudding so hard she thought she might be sick. Once she stepped over the threshold there would be no going back.

Chapter Seven
TABLINUM

Later that night, Juba heard Ursula's voice at the door of his bedroom.

'Boys! Wake up!' she cried.

'*Boys! Wake up!*' echoed Loquax.

Juba kept his eyes shut. He had been dreaming of their villa in Rome on a hot summer's day.

In the dream, his mother had been sitting cross-legged before her loom, singing as she wove. On a small carpet beside her, baby Dora lay on her tummy. She had arched her back and raised her big head and was gurgling happily as she tried to grasp a rag doll that was just out of reach.

Juba did not have to open his eyes to know he was not in Rome. He was in the cold, grey province of Britannia and he could hear the rain still falling steadily, making a symphony of sound as it struck roof tile and gutter, leaf and earth. He could hear the creak of leather webbing as Prasutus got up from the bed next to his.

'Come on, Juba!' urged his sister from the doorway. 'Everyone's in the tablinum!'

Juba kept his eyes firmly closed.

Had he also dreamt his night encounter with Bouda in the peristyle?

No. He groaned as he remembered what he had said to Bouda about the Minerva gem. He had planned to give it to Bouda as a betrothal gift, but how could he do that if she already considered it to be hers?

He had gone about it all wrong.

He groaned again and pulled the blanket over his head.

'Juba!' Ursula's voice was sharp. 'You must come now. Flavia Gemina is here. And Doctor Jonathan! They have bad news.'

'*Bad news!*' echoed Loquax.

Juba was up in an instant. Perhaps the thunder and lightning *had* been a warning sign.

He was the last to arrive and found the others already there. Flavia Gemina, their patroness, was sitting in Caudex's leather chair behind an oak table in the lamplit tablinum. Her light brown hair, usually piled up in a tower of curls, was done in a simple bun at the back of her neck in the old Republican style. Caudex stood on her left and her friend Doctor Jonathan on her right, his damp cloak steaming in the heat of a brazier.

All three of them looked graver than Juba had ever seen them.

Bouda and Prasutus were already there. Prasutus yawning. Bouda pale and trembling. Juba wanted to put a comforting arm around her shoulders, but had to satisfy himself with standing close beside her.

'My dear ones,' said Flavia Gemina, 'I have come to tell you in person that you must leave Britannia at once.'

'It's my fault, isn't it?' said Ursula. 'Because of what I said to the governor.'

'No,' said Flavia. 'Although you must guard your lips in future.' She took a deep breath. 'When we got back to Londinium, my husband and the governor and I went through all recent correspondence. We found this.' She held up a sheet of papyrus with official-looking writing on it and a seal at the bottom. 'It is dated two months ago. The governor gets so many missives. Somehow this one escaped my notice. It mentions that the Emperor has sent one of his most feared freedmen to capture three child fugitives: the children of Lucius Domitius Ursus.'

'Tell them his name,' said Doctor Jonathan grimly.

Flavia closed her eyes for a moment and then opened them. 'The Emperor's freedman goes by a single name: Tortor.'

Juba felt a thrill of horror.

'I am still learning Latin,' said Prasutus. 'Tortor means "torturer", doesn't it?'

'Yes,' said Flavia. 'I'm afraid so.'

'Father mentioned him once.' Juba said. 'Is he the one who uses a red-hot poker to . . .?'

Flavia Gemina held up her hand to stop him. 'Yes. Yes, he does. That is why you must leave here at once. You are all in danger. Furthermore, we are putting Caudex and his family in danger too.'

Juba nodded. 'We'll leave right away,' he said and looked at Caudex. 'We don't want to endanger anyone.'

'I wish I could do more to help.' Flavia Gemina was blinking back tears. 'But my husband and I are responsible for a household of five adults and seven children. No, eight. Nubia and Aristo have just had a little girl. Their fourth child.' She took a deep breath and looked up. 'This time I can't even give you a token of passage. But what I can give you is a companion. Jonathan has agreed to go with you.' She gestured to Doctor Jonathan standing beside her.

'*Euge!* Yay!' squealed Ursula. She ran behind the desk to hug the doctor's waist.

'She wants me to teach her to be an animal doctor,' Jonathan explained to a startled Flavia.

'But where shall we go?' asked Juba. 'If we can't stay in Britannia and we can't go home to Italy . . .'

'Did the twins already set sail for Rome?' Doctor Jonathan asked Flavia Gemina.

She nodded. 'They were due to set sail the day before yesterday, from Londinium.'

'Too bad,' he murmured. 'We could have sailed with them and disembarked at any one of a dozen ports along the way.'

'You'll have to arrange other transport,' said Flavia. She gave Jonathan two gold coins. 'This is all I can spare. It should get you passage on another ship.' She held up both hands, palms forward. 'But don't tell me where you're going. If I don't know then I can't lie when the governor questions me.' She sighed and forced a smile. 'However, I can tell you that your brother Fronto's cohort crossed the channel two days ago and are safely on their way to Colonia.'

Juba touched the bronze Mercury down the front of his tunic and breathed a prayer of thanks.

'What about me?' said Prasutus. 'And Bouda? Should we go, too?'

Juba glanced at Bouda, but her profile did not betray anything.

'You two can blend in more easily than Juba and Ursula,' said Flavia after a moment, 'so I don't think you need to leave this province. But you must leave Verulamium.'

'Prasutus, you have to come with us!' cried Ursula. 'And you, too, Bouda,' she added quickly. Then she looked up at Doctor Jonathan. 'Can they come with us?'

Jonathan gave a single nod. 'If they want to come then they are most welcome.'

Flavia Gemina's chair scraped as she stood up. 'I'm sorry,' she said. 'But you must hurry. We don't have a moment to lose.'

Juba turned to ask Bouda if she would come with them. But she was already hurrying out of the tablinum.

He caught up with her at the door of her bedroom and clutched her arm to make her turn and face him.

'What?' The intensity of her gaze made him step back.

'Are you coming with us?' he stammered.

'Do you want me to come?'

He wanted to tell her that of course she must come. That he couldn't imagine life without her. That he wanted to marry her and that he intended to give her the Minerva gem as a wedding gift.

Instead he said, 'It might be best if you leave this province for a while. If the governor finds out you're Boudica's great-granddaughter he might feel it's his duty to tell the Emperor.'

'And you?' She lifted her chin a little. 'Do you want me to come with you?'

This was the perfect moment to tell her how he felt.

'Yes, I do,' he said softly. Then he took a deep breath. 'Bouda, in the past few months—'

A man's hand on his shoulder made him jump. 'Don't just stand there talking!' said Doctor Jonathan ben Mordecai. 'Get packing!'

Chapter Eight
ANIMALIA

It only took Ursula a quarter of an hour to collect all her belongings.

Apart from a cormorant-feather cloak that she was leaving behind, she put on all the clothes she owned: a wine-red woollen tunic over a nettle-cloth undertunic, then a woven belt with a leather pouch for coins and a knife in a leather sheath. Over this went her pine-green woollen cloak. It had a hood and was fastened with a bronze and enamel fibula shaped like a running dog, a gift from the chieftain of a Belgic village where they had stayed the previous winter. She wore felt house-slippers under slightly too-big boots that Bouda had outgrown. Down the front of her tunic she carried a folding spoon wrapped in a napkin. Loquax the mynah bird was safely stowed in his covered wicker cage where he could not blurt treason. Big Gartha, the faithful scent-hound, padded beside her.

But she was missing one pet, her beloved cat. Ursula had adopted Meer while fleeing Rome. The tiny kitten had been near death, but Ursula had revived her with milk from a baby's beaker. The kitten had spent the first six weeks of her life on board a ship, clinging to Ursula's left shoulder. When she became too big to ride on her mistress's shoulder, she often draped herself around

Ursula's neck like a fur stole. But in the past nine months, she had taken to domestic life.

Caudex's Roman-style house provided her with two courtyards to explore, as well as the stables and the woods. There were mice to catch, bowls of cream to lap and little Fortunata to entertain her with a piece of string.

That was where Ursula finally found Meer, curled up at the foot of Fortunata's cot.

When she came into the little girl's room, the cat lifted her head and blinked inscrutable slate-grey eyes.

Ursula took a deep breath. 'Meer,' she whispered. 'A bad man is after us and we have to run away. We're going on another sea voyage and then a long journey by land to see Fronto. I would love you to come with me. But it will be very dangerous and I know you're happy here in Caudex's villa, so if you want to stay, you can.'

Ursula paused and then spoke in a firm and confident tone. 'Meer! To me!'

A year ago, this would have brought Meer instantly to her shoulder.

Now her cat merely stretched and jumped down on to the floor. For a few moments she wove back and forth between Ursula's legs, purring loudly. Then she sat on the polished wooden floor and began to clean her left leg.

Ursula scooped up Meer and put her on her shoulder.

For a moment the cat stayed there, purring, then she jumped back down.

Ursula swallowed hard. 'All right, Meer. If that's what you want.'

For the last time she hugged her grown-up kitten. 'I love you, Meer!' she whispered and her tears made the soft fur wet. Beside her, Gartha whined softly.

At last Ursula put Meer down. Then, holding the covered birdcage and followed by her faithful hound, she hurried out of the villa before her resolve melted.

Next she had to say farewell to the oxen and horses.

As she entered the dimly lit stable, she saw Doctor Jonathan and Flavia Gemina.

They were arguing.

'Why won't you?' Flavia Gemina's voice was low but angry. 'Those children spent months trying to find you! Ursula nearly died!'

'I didn't ask you to send out search parties for me,' he replied. 'Why do you think I've been travelling under another name? It's because I didn't want to be found.'

'By me?' She sounded hurt.

'By anybody!'

'But, shared with the right people, that information could end a reign of terror!'

'I've sworn twice not to harm another person,' said Doctor Jonathan. 'Once in the Hippocratic oath and once to my God. Remember what I told you the first time we met? Our Lord tells us to love our enemies.'

'You and your ridiculous God!' she cried.

Ursula's foot crunched some straw and they both turned their heads.

Flavia Gemina moved towards her, both hands extended. 'Dear Ursula,' she said. 'I'm so sorry to send you away like this.' Her hands were cold when she gripped Ursula's.

'Don't worry, domina,' said Ursula bravely. 'Doctor Jonathan is my new patron. He's teaching me to be an animal doctor, and how to follow the Way. And he can do that anywhere.'

Jonathan put his arm around Ursula's shoulders and gave her

a reassuring squeeze. 'She reminds me of you, when you were young,' he said to Flavia.

Flavia shook her head. 'Poor Jonathan!' she said. 'To be saddled with another headstrong girl!' Then she bent close to Ursula and whispered in her ear, 'You're good for him. But you must guard your tongue or you'll get him killed.'

Ursula gave a solemn nod. Then she noticed movement in the gloom at the far end of the stables. Caudex and Prasutus had come in and were going to the oxen. 'Are we taking the oxen and the carruca?' she asked the doctor. 'And the ponies?'

'Too dangerous to take the carruca,' said Jonathan. 'People might recognise it. So we're only taking the ox-cart, and only as far as—' He saw Flavia's face and stopped abruptly. 'We're only taking the ox-cart on the first stage of our journey. Then Caudex will drive it back here. Juba has agreed to give the animals to Caudex as thanks for hosting us all winter.'

Ursula nodded. 'I've left Meer as a present for Fortunata. It's sad the animals can't come with us, but I'm happy that they will live here with Caudex.' She turned to one of the ponies and said, 'You've been happy here, haven't you?'

The pony dipped his head and gave a soft snort, which Ursula took for *yes*.

Flavia Gemina said, 'It is kind of you and Juba to give Caudex the ponies and those two fine oxen.'

'It's the least we can do,' said Juba, coming into the stable. 'He let the six of us stay here all winter. That's quite a few mouths to feed. I've also given him one of Pater's rubies,' he added.

Ursula felt more tears coming. She went into the ponies' stalls and told them how much she loved them and how much she would miss them. And she wept into the long silky manes that she had brushed every morning.

Presently she felt a hand on her back. 'Ursula, we have to go!' It was Prasutus. 'Everyone else is waiting,' he said.

He held Loquax's covered cage and Gartha stood at his side.

'Oh, Prasutus!' she cried. 'I'll miss them so much! And Meer!' She buried her face in his rust-red woollen cloak and when he gave her a comforting hug she could feel him trembling. If brave Prasutus was worried, it must be bad. So she dried her tears and followed him outside, resting one hand lightly on Gartha's shoulders.

The fiery smear of the rising sun was about to be swallowed by dark clouds that promised more rain. But for the moment it cast a strange pink glow over villa and farmyard.

Flavia was giving Juba an extra-long hug and whispering something in his ear. Ursula saw that he was fighting back tears. When Bouda came forward, Flavia also whispered something in the British girl's ear.

Ursula was hoping for a word, too, and she was not disappointed. Flavia kissed her forehead, stroked Gartha's woolly head and then bent forward and spoke in a low voice. 'Never lose your boldness and your compassion, dear Ursula. They are your gifts. But remember . . .' She pressed her forefinger to her lips in the sign for silence.

Ursula nodded and tried not to cry. With Gartha at one side and Prasutus on the other, she turned to follow the ox-cart, which was already moving up the muddy path towards the main road.

At the end of the drive they turned and waved one last time to their patroness. Flavia Gemina stood alone in the strange pink dawn, the chill breeze making her blue palla flutter around her.

When they turned on to the road that would take them to the east coast of Britannia, Ursula felt her heart break. She would miss Caudex and his wife and little Fortunata. She would miss her faithful oxen and the beloved ponies too.

But most of all she would miss her grown-up kitten, Meer.

As fresh tears welled up she told herself that it was for the best. After all, they were being pursued by a man called the Torturer. At least Meer would be safe.

Sometimes love meant letting go.

Chapter Nine
FAENUM

With every step they took that day, Bouda thanked Minerva that she had not been caught trying to flee the villa.

A few hours earlier she had been in the very act of lifting the bolt from its cradle when a pounding on the other side of the door – only a few inches away – almost made her faint.

At first she had thought it was soldiers come to arrest them, but when she heard familiar voices calling for Caudex she lifted up the bolt and opened the double doors to Flavia Gemina and Doctor Jonathan. They stood wet and shivering from having travelled the last few miles from Londinium in a two-man raeda pulled by a long-suffering mule.

If she had opened the doors a moment earlier, they would have caught her.

Once they arrived she couldn't very well run away, with the entire household awake and Caudex lighting torches and Flavia asking them to come to the tablinum.

And then Flavia's parting words had struck her like a bolt of lightning.

Maybe Juba *did* love her.

Maybe she had a chance to win his respect.

It was a miserable day, with steady rain and icy puddles.

The only good thing about it was that most people were staying inside their houses. Nor was it a market day, so they had passed through Verulamium unnoticed.

By midday Bouda had blisters on both heels, damp clothes and a runny nose.

They stopped for a few hours in the early evening to let the oxen rest, but then the sky cleared and a half moon rose and lit the road, so Jonathan and Prasutus took over driving. The others bedded down in the hay beneath a sheet of tarred linen stretched across the open top of the wagon. They rolled up in their cloaks and lay next to each other like piglets nursing from a sow, with Bouda between Ursula and Juba, and Caudex snoring on Juba's other side. It reminded Bouda of the nights when she had huddled with other child cutpurses in a small room with only one brazier for warmth.

In this case Gartha acted as a brazier: a warm, reassuring bulk lying at their feet. But despite the scent-hound's warmth, Bouda was still shivering.

Ursula was soon snoring like Caudex, but Bouda couldn't fall asleep; the hay cart was too cold and noisy. She turned to see if Juba was awake. Faint silver moonlight seeping through a chink between the tarpaulin and one side of the juddering wagon showed the gleam of his eyes in the darkness.

'Are you awake?' he whispered, barely audible above the grinding of the ox-cart wheels.

'Yes.'

'Are you frightened?'

'No,' she replied, 'I'm too damp and cold. And I think there are fleas in this hay. Juba,' she said after a pause, 'what did Flavia Gemina say to you before we left?'

He gave a bitter snort of laughter. 'She told me not to carry

51

the burdens of the world on my shoulders. But how can I not? It was my mother's dying wish that I save the children. And I failed.'

'Your mother didn't mean you should save all the children in the world. She only meant Ursula and Fronto. And you did save them.'

'My mother meant baby Dora too. And as you pointed out, I sold her to pay for our passage.'

Bouda felt a pang of remorse. 'I'm sorry I said that,' she whispered. 'You did what you had to do. How could you take a five-month-old baby on a six-week sea voyage? How were you supposed to feed her? Where would you get milk?'

'There was a goat on board,' Juba said. 'Although it did get washed overboard during a storm.'

'See?' she said. 'You did the right thing. And you found a woman who will be a loving foster mother.'

'Yes. Calpurnia Firma promised to love her to the tips of her fingers. But Dora was my own flesh and blood. My baby sister.'

The cart was going over a noisy bit of road, so Bouda brought her mouth closer to Juba's ear.

'Juba,' she whispered after a moment, 'don't you want to go back to Rome?'

'With all my heart,' he said. 'I want to see if baby Dora is happy and well. But if we went back and the Emperor's men caught us they might hurt Dora too. And her new family.'

'What if the Emperor should die?' she said. 'And a new one came to power? A kind one?'

'Then I'd fly back like an arrow from the bow.' There was a pause and then he said, 'Would you come with us? To Rome, I mean?'

His question gave her renewed hope that he cared. 'Yes,' she said. 'You know it's my dream to visit Rome.'

'It's strange,' he said. 'You're British but you love all things Roman. Ursula is Roman and loves all things British.'

'Don't forget,' whispered Bouda, 'my grandfather might have been a legionary with the Second Augusta, so I could have Roman blood. And I don't know who my father was. He might have been Roman too.'

'Your hair and skin prove you are at least part British,' he murmured.

'My hair may be British but my soul must be Roman,' she sighed. 'I would give almost anything for an hour in the steam room of a bath-house!'

'You might get your wish,' whispered Juba. 'Caudex says we should reach Camulodunum tomorrow around noon. He knows of a good tavern with soft beds and a bath-house.'

'Oh, Juba! A hot bath and a warm bed would be so good! But can we afford it?'

'Yes. I have enough coins for a room in an inn and a visit to the baths. And I still have three gems left. One of them is an emerald that should fund our journey to Colonia.' He paused and then added, 'Flavia Gemina told me something else.'

'What?'

Juba's voice was so low that she could barely hear him. 'She asked me to find out what Doctor Jonathan's information is. The knowledge he has that could depose Domitian.'

'Oh! I know what it is.'

'You do?'

'Yes. He told Ursula, and she told me. Apparently he knows the exact time and date of Domitian's death, as predicted by his astrologer.'

'When?'

'I don't know that. Only that it's some time this year.'

'We've got to make him tell us,' muttered Juba. 'We could use that information to find out when it's safe to return to Rome.'

They were quiet for a moment. Then Juba whispered, 'What did Flavia Gemina tell you?'

'When?'

'When she said goodbye to each of us.'

'Oh. She told me to seek the highest good,' said Bouda.

'Ah. The motto of the Epicureans. What else? She said more than a few words to you.'

'I can't tell you. It was personal.'

'I just shared something personal with you,' he said.

'I know, but this is different . . . I can't.'

She could tell that her refusal to share hurt him, and after a moment's silence he turned his back on her.

Bouda sighed. But there was no way she could repeat Flavia's words. Words that made her glad she had not run away.

'*Dear Bouda*,' Flavia had whispered, '*I can tell that Juba loves you. But he also loves what is good and noble. If you want to earn his love, you must seek the highest good.*'

Chapter Ten
BOVES

Ursula would never forget what happened in the port of Camulodunum.

It was around noon and raining lightly when the ox-cart reached the outskirts of Britannia's oldest Roman town. She and Bouda sat either side of Caudex on the driver's bench, while Juba and Gartha walked on the road beside the cart. Doctor Jonathan and Prasutus were asleep on the damp bed of hay; they had taken the early shift of driving.

As they crested a low rise in the road, Ursula saw something like a giant's spear rising above a line of trees on the horizon. It was the huge crane leaning over the half-built circus.

Juba lifted his chin towards the massive crane. 'That reminds me,' he said. 'You're famous there on account of your exploits last year.'

Ursula nodded. Although nearly nine months had passed, she knew she would probably be recognised by any of the two thousand people who had seen her fly above Camulodunum's half-built racecourse.

Juba called up to Caudex. 'Can we get to the port without entering the town?'

'What about the hot bath you promised me, Juba?' slurred

Bouda. She was leaning against Caudex with her eyes half closed. 'It's my heart's desire.'

'Bouda, you should try to sleep on the straw with Prasutus and Doctor Jonathan,' said Ursula.

Bouda shook her head. 'The straw is full of fleas,' she murmured. 'And they prefer me to any of you.'

'Here's the road to the port,' said Caudex. He twitched the reins to make the oxen take a muddy fork heading northeast. 'We'll find you a bath-house,' he said to Bouda.

'Salvete, Juba and Ursula!' called a voice from the road. 'You'd better hurry: the tide is almost on the turn.'

It took a moment for Ursula to realise she was not dreaming.

'What did you say?' called Juba.

The young man turned his mule and pulled back the hood of his cloak.

'Don't you recognise me?' he called. 'You sailed with me a few years ago.'

'Bubo!' cried Ursula. 'It's Bubo!' She put her hand on Caudex's arm and he pulled the oxen to a halt.

Ursula felt a smile spread across her face. Bubo had been the youngest sailor on board the ship they had taken from Ostia.

He was now two inches taller and had a short brown beard.

Juba was frowning. 'If the tide is about to turn, why are you going that way?'

'I dreamt of a bad storm at sea,' said the youth, 'and decided to stay here in Britannia, where I was born. If you want to catch the *Centaur*, you'd better hurry.' He grinned at Gartha. 'Put a saddle on that dog and ride as fast as you can!' He turned his mule, kicked her into motion and called back, 'Farewell!'

'What's the centaur?' asked Bouda sleepily.

'The *Centaur* is the name of Castor's ship!' cried Ursula.

'I thought they sailed from Londinium at the beginning of the week,' said Bouda.

'They did,' said Ursula. 'But this must be one of the ports they visit.'

'This is an answer to prayer!' cried Juba. 'If we can get to the port in time we might get free passage across the sea to Gallia. I'll run ahead and tell them to wait!'

His tawny cloak flapped behind him as he ran up the muddy road towards the tops of masts rising behind some trees. Gartha loped after him until they reached the brow of the hill. Then the dog stopped and looked back at her mistress.

Ursula reckoned the port was half a mile away. Could Juba make it?

Caudex flicked the oxen with his whip and they moved forward more quickly than any time since they set out. Suddenly Volens – the right-hand ox – stumbled, making the cart lurch to a violent stop.

Ursula jumped off the cart and ran to Volens.

'What's happening?' asked Doctor Jonathan, sitting up and blinking. He had hay in his curly dark hair. Prasutus was awake now too.

'The twins' ship might be here,' said Bouda. 'The tide is almost on the turn but if we can get to the port in time we might get free passage to the mainland.'

Down on the ground, Ursula looked up from examining the lame ox's right foreleg. 'It's his bad hoof,' she called to them. 'Volens is willing but he's not able.' She pointed at a blacksmith's stall they had passed a little earlier. 'Maybe that blacksmith can make him a sandal out of iron.'

'No time if the tide is about to turn!' Doctor Jonathan used his walking stick to ease himself off the back of the cart. He turned to Caudex, who had just come down from the front of the cart. 'With all this mud it will be just as fast for us to go on foot from here,' he said. 'And if you turn back now, nobody will link you to us.'

Caudex pondered this for a moment, and then nodded and guided Volens and Potens to the side of the road where the ground was drier. While the others said goodbye to Caudex, Ursula hugged the necks of her beloved oxen. 'Thank you for pulling us so diligently,' she told them. 'You have been willing and able.' She kissed their velvety noses.

Bouda was the last to say goodbye to Caudex. Ursula was surprised to hear her say, 'The past nine months have been the happiest time of my life.'

Caudex was weeping. 'I'll miss you too, Lady Bouda. And so will little Fortunata.' He wiped his eyes with his sleeve and looked at Ursula. 'She'll miss you both!'

Ursula gave Caudex a fierce hug and then lingered on the verge; she wanted to make sure he reached the blacksmith's shop.

'Ursula! Bouda! Hurry!' cried Prasutus. She turned to see that he and Doctor Jonathan had joined Gartha at the crest of the hill and were looking back at her.

Doctor Jonathan cupped his hands around his mouth to direct his voice. 'We can see the twins on a ship!' he called. 'And Juba running towards them!'

'They're beckoning us!' yelled Prasutus. 'They seem— Oh no!'

'What?' Ursula grabbed her birdcage and ran after Bouda.

'Look!' Jonathan pointed. 'Soldiers.'

As Ursula reached the top of the hill, she could see about fifty helmets moving through the crowds that thronged the harbour. 'Maybe they're here on business,' she said.

'Yes.' Doctor Jonathan gripped his walking stick so tightly that his knuckles turned white. 'I think their business is arresting us.'

Prasutus turned to them, his flushed cheeks almost as red as his hair. 'You three go. I'll distract them.'

'Prasutus, no!' cried Ursula.

'Yes.' He gave her a quick kiss on the forehead. 'You get on board the *Centaur*. I'll try to get a boat to row me out to you once they're gone. The soldiers probably have descriptions of all of you, but they don't know me. Don't worry,' he said, when he saw the expression on Ursula's face. 'I'll see you again.'

But he was wrong.

Chapter Eleven
TORTOR

'What's Prasutus doing?' cried Juba as he ran back to the others. 'Castor and Raven can take us, but we have to go now!' Then he saw the helmets and his heart plunged into his stomach. 'Oh no! Are those soldiers here for us?'

'We don't know!' said Ursula. 'Prasutus is going to distract them while we get on board!'

Doctor Jonathan put up the hood of his nutmeg-coloured cloak. 'Let's hurry. But don't run or we'll attract their attention.'

Juba nodded grimly, then turned to lead the way. He could see one of the *Centaur*'s crew untying mooring ropes and Castor and Raven standing ready to raise the gangplank. If they missed the tide they would be trapped in the harbour for another eight hours, with no way to evade the soldiers. Like the doctor and Ursula, Juba had put up the hood of his cloak. Bouda's cloak had a fur collar but no hood, so she had wrapped her leaf-green palla around her copper hair.

Juba glanced to the left and saw Prasutus's distinctive rust-red hooded cloak reach the soldiers' bright helmets. Touching the small bronze Mercury down the front of his tunic, Juba prayed that the god of travellers would protect him.

'Come on!' Castor was leaning over the ship's balustrade.

'Before the tide and the wind turn against us!'

Doctor Jonathan stood aside to let Bouda and Ursula go up the gangplank first. But Gartha did not like the look of the slippery, moving board. Ursula had to come back down and tug her collar while Doctor Jonathan pushed from behind.

A few other ships were already out on the open sea. The *Centaur* was the only ship still trying to leave the harbour.

At last they got Gartha on board.

'Come on!' Doctor Jonathan looked down at Juba from the top of the gangplank. He was leaning on his walking stick with his left hand and stretching out his right.

'Just a moment,' said Juba. 'I just want to make sure Prasutus is all right.'

'You'll have a better view from up here.'

Juba looked for Prasutus's rust-red cloak, but had lost sight of him among the throng of sailors, dockers and merchants.

Turning back to the ship, he saw that Castor and Raven were already raising the gangplank. He had to leap to make it on to the slippery piece of wood.

He almost fell back but managed to catch the end of the doctor's outstretched walking stick.

'By all the gods!' he gasped as he tumbled on to the deck. He stood up and glared at the twins. But their faces were pale and Raven was pointing back towards the wharf. Standing near the soldiers and Prasutus was a man in a black hooded tunic.

'Did you see his face?' asked Castor.

'It's terrifying,' said Raven.

Juba shook his head.

'Up here!' Ursula was already up in the rigging. 'Juba, you can see from up here!'

Juba used a rope to pull himself up the mast to the yardarm, the horizontal beam of wood that held the sail. Ursula's feet were resting on the rolled-up sail and her arms held the polished wood. 'I think Prasutus is in trouble,' she said, moving further along to make room for him. 'Can you see the hooded man's face?'

Juba shook his head. From up here, he had a clear view but the hooded man was speaking to Prasutus and still had his back to them.

The throng of people on the dock sensed that something was happening and had come to watch. Some of them had crowded closer and others had moved back to form a circular space containing Black Hood, Prasutus and fifty or so soldiers standing behind him.

For a while Prasutus spoke and the cloaked figure nodded his head.

Then there was a commotion in the crowd. A lavender litter carried by eight slaves came trotting up. The litter-bearers set it down and after a moment the curtains parted and a fat Roman emerged from it. Of all the people on the dock, he was the only one wearing a toga.

'Oh no!' murmured Juba. 'Isn't that Montanus?'

'Yes!' cried Ursula and turned to Juba with fear in her eyes. 'And he knows who Prasutus is! Remember? He saw us together in the legate's villa after the games last year?'

Fat Montanus had entered the circle of action and was pointing at Prasutus.

In response, Prasutus shook his head vigorously. Then he pointed away from the harbour towards the town and the giant crane. He was obviously trying to put them off the track.

Montanus took the bait. The fat man shaded his eyes and peered towards Camulodunum.

But Black Hood was not fooled. Instead of looking in the direction Prasutus was pointing, he slowly turned to look in the exact opposite direction. Towards the *Centaur*, which was finally moving out of her berth.

Juba gaped.

The hooded man wore a gilded mask such as cavalry officers wore. Or Charon, the executioner in the games. There was something chilling about the smooth gold face with its empty eyeholes. Even from this distance, those terrible black eyes seemed to find him.

Juba wanted to make the sign against evil but he needed both hands to cling to the yardarm. 'Dear gods, protect us!' he whispered.

'Juba!' cried Ursula. 'That must be the man Flavia Gemina was telling us about. The one sent to hunt us down.'

'Tortor,' said Juba. 'The Torturer.' And for the first time he noticed the thing in the hooded man's hand. It was an iron rod, the sort used to stir hot coals in an oven or on a grill. At gladiatorial games, a man dressed as Charon used a red-hot poker like that to prod fallen gladiators in order to see if they were really dead.

As if his thought had given the Torturer this very idea, the masked man pointed and a moment later two soldiers brought him a brazier of hot coals from a stall selling grilled fish. The hooded man put the iron poker into the coals.

'By Jupiter!' muttered Juba. 'If they torture Prasutus he'll give us all away. They might even make him betray Caudex. And Flavia Gemina!'

'Prasutus would never betray us!' cried Ursula fiercely.

'There are few things more painful than being branded,' came Doctor Jonathan's voice from the deck below them. 'Torture always works, because even the bravest man is only flesh and blood.'

Juba felt dizzy and took a deep breath to calm himself.

Over on the docks, Tortor gave another command.

The crowd parted as most of the soldiers jogged towards an oared warship that lay low in the water.

An oared warship! As long as they were in the shelter of the harbour, such a ship could easily catch them.

'By Epona!' cried a voice from the other end of the yardarm. It was one of the sailors. 'Either help us release the mainsail or get out of the way!'

Ursula was moving up the mast to the lookout's perch. Juba did not have her head for heights, but he needed to see what was happening so he followed her up. A year and a half ago he could have gone up as quickly as a monkey, but he was heavier now – more muscular in his belly and thighs – and his arms and legs were trembling by the time he reached her. The lookout's platform was a disc of wood with less than six feet of slender mast above it.

It was barely big enough for one, and dangerously cramped for two.

Juba managed to wedge his feet on the tiny circular platform beside Ursula's, and his hands touched hers as they both clung to the polished wood mast, not much thicker than his wrist at this height.

The oared warship had already cast off and it was manoeuvring out of its berth. In a moment it would be skimming towards them.

Meanwhile, two soldiers remained on the wharf, holding Prasutus by the arms. Montanus and Tortor were with him too. As the torturer brought the glowing poker out of its bed of coals,

Juba felt sick. The pain would be unimaginable. Not even the bravest warrior in the Empire would be able to resist it. Prasutus would betray everyone who had ever helped them.

'Dear God, please save him!' Ursula cried.

Somehow, her prayer was answered.

Using a technique that Caudex had taught them, Prasutus did a backwards somersault. This brought down the two soldiers holding his arms. They crashed on to the dock with a clang so loud that even those on board the *Centaur* heard it. Then Prasutus dived for Montanus, grabbed the hem of his toga and tugged. With a squeal the fat man toppled over, then rolled across the dock like a reel of yarn unspooling. Tortor lunged at the boy with his glowing poker, but Prasutus was a natural acrobat and Caudex had taught him well. Jumping nimbly to one side, he tossed the fat man's enormous toga over his attacker. Howling with rage, Tortor flailed and flapped, finally blundering into the brazier. As he knocked it over he sent hot coals and people scattering.

With all four of his captors down and the remaining soldiers still unaware of what had just happened, Prasutus ran. As he pelted through the cheering throng of people, Juba saw him toss away his distinctive fox-red cloak. A moment later, a bushy-moustached Briton handed him a rough brown paenula, like a runner passing the baton in a relay.

Prasutus put it on and slowed to a fast walk. Juba was able to track him for a moment but soon lost sight of him. Dozens of other Britons wore identical cloaks.

Juba breathed a sigh of relief.

Below him, the sailors were still struggling to set the mainsail. Juba let himself down and managed to help them by untying the last rope.

As the mainsail slowly unfurled and then filled, Juba felt the ship come alive. The sailors cheered and Juba guessed that once they were out in the choppy waves they would be safe.

A huge sense of relief flooded Juba and he felt like shouting with joy.

Doctor Jonathan and the twins stood at the stern, looking back at the ever-receding warship and punching the air in exultation. Soon Ursula and the sailors joined them, some shouting insults at their pursuers. Only Bouda stood alone at the prow. The wind whipped her cloak and tunic, and it tangled her copper hair.

As Juba jumped down on to the deck with a thump, she looked over her shoulder at him. Her face was pale and her eyes haunted, but to him she had never looked more beautiful.

The joy he had suppressed was transformed into something else: courage. He was embarking on a dangerous mission and she had decided to come with him. This was surely the moment to tell her he loved her and wanted to marry her, and that the Minerva gem was hers to keep whether she accepted his proposal or not.

Juba strode forward across the bucking deck and felt joy drench him along with the sea spray.

But when he was only a few paces from Bouda, she turned and ran away.

Chapter Twelve
NAUSEA

The moment the merchant ship *Centaur* moved out of its berth, Bouda began to feel sick.

While the others gathered at the back of the ship or up in the rigging to see what was happening to Prasutus, all she could think about was her churning stomach. And when the sail unfurled and caught the wind she felt she might vomit. She didn't want anyone to see, so she moved to the front of the ship.

For a moment the nausea subsided and she almost dared to hope she would not disgrace herself. Then the ship moved out of the relative shelter of the harbour and into big, choppy waves. The deck began to rise and fall. She could taste bitter bile at the back of her throat and swallowed hard.

Shouts of triumph came from above her; she hoped they were for Prasutus. She turned to look at the horizon ahead, and took deep breaths. But the nausea was getting worse, not better. Presently, a big cheer made her turn to look back. Everyone was waving or shaking their fists at something. All except for Juba. He was walking towards her.

He had a strange look on his face. He was smiling and his eyes never left hers as he moved forward on the bucking deck.

For the ship was like an untamed horse now: rearing up and then falling away beneath them.

Now Juba was close to her, his smiling mouth open as he started to speak. But she never heard what he had to say. She bolted to the rail and made it just in time. Miserably she hung over it and voided the contents of her stomach. She was sick again and again, retching even when there was nothing to bring up.

A small part of her was ashamed that Juba had seen her weakness. Her animal nature had been revealed to him. He could see that she was neither good nor noble. But that barely mattered. All she wanted was release from this misery. She felt warm hands on her shoulders and heard Juba's voice in her ear. 'At least you went to the leeside.'

She had no idea what he was talking about. Groaning, she slumped down on to the deck. The sodden planks of wood were cold but strangely comforting. She pressed her cheek against them and whimpered.

'Bouda,' came his voice. 'Bouda, you can't stay there.'

'Why not?' she managed to moan.

'You'll catch a fever. Come on. Stand up. You'll feel better in a while. Captain Caerulus says the crossing only takes half a day.'

She groaned at the thought of another half hour of this, much less half a day.

Then a new wave of nausea rose up in her. She managed to get to her knees to be sick over a lower part of the rail. The second bout of heaves left her feeling so exhausted that when she lay down again she actually slept. But the relief did not last long. Perhaps a quarter of an hour later she was heaving again. The ship was bucking even more and a wave drenched her in icy foam. The fur trim of her cloak was soaked and gave no comfort.

'Minerva, help me!' she whispered through chattering teeth and clutched the gem on its leather thong.

Juba's voice said, 'Here. Drink this.' She felt the nozzle of a waterskin against her lips and gratefully sucked posca, water tinted with vinegar. It made her feel a little better.

'There's a brazier in the captain's hut,' said Juba. 'It will warm you.'

'No.' She gave her head a feeble shake. 'Can't move.'

'At least come and dry your clothes.'

'No.' This time she didn't even have the strength to shake her head.

He sighed. 'I suppose it doesn't matter. Everything will get wet soon enough.'

She groaned and rolled over on her back. Up above she could see swollen clouds and ropes and Ursula beaming down at her from a lofty part of the rigging. 'Oh,' she groaned again. 'Am I the only one who's sick?'

'No.' He glanced sideways and she turned her head to see Gartha lying miserably on the deck a few paces away. The dog was breathing fast, her flank going in and out like a blacksmith's bellows pumping double-time.

'Poor Gartha,' Bouda murmured. Then another wave of sickness overwhelmed her and she brought up the posca he had given her. He gently held her hair away from her face.

'Juba, do you care about me?'

A momentary pause and then he said, 'Very much.'

'Will you do something for me?'

A longer pause. 'Yes.'

'Swear it!' She made herself sit up.

'What?'

She wiped her mouth and sat with her back against the low

69

rail and breathed in fast little sips like Gartha. She fought back nausea, reached into the neck of her tartan tunic and pulled out the priceless gem on its sturdy leather thong. 'Swear on this. Swear by the goddess Minerva!'

'But I don't know what you want me to do!'

'If you care about me, swear it!'

'All right.' His warm brown hand closed over her icy fingers and the gem. 'I swear by the goddess Minerva I will do whatever you ask.'

She closed her eyes. 'Promise you'll never take me on a ship again.'

There was a long pause. 'I can't promise that.'

'But you swore!'

'You shouldn't have made me swear.'

Anger mixed with the nausea in her stomach. She opened her eyes. 'But what does it even matter? We're about to land and go and find Fronto. We never have to go on a ship again.'

He looked away, his eyes almost pure grey in this light. 'We're not going to Colonia,' he said after a moment. 'We're going to Ostia.'

'What? But last night you said you couldn't go back to Rome.'

'I said that because I was afraid.' He looked at her. 'But seeing what that torturer almost did to Prasutus . . . it made me so angry. And then finding the *Centaur* ready and waiting to take us to Rome. It was like a sign from the gods. I'm tired of running. I'm going to get the doctor to tell us the information he's been keeping to himself so we can bring down the tyrant.' His hand squeezed around hers.

'But what about the danger? You said going to Ostia would be like going to the lion's den. You said your presence might put Dora's new family at risk.'

'But look!' He spread his hands. 'Here we are on a ship bound for Ostia, the very place where Dora is living. Maybe the gods want me to return.'

Bouda groaned and let her head fall back against the low rail that protected the deck. 'How many days will it take us to get there?'

'I think you mean how many weeks. Six. At least.'

'Six weeks?' She lifted her head and stared at him in horror. 'Over forty days?'

'I'm afraid so.'

'And you can't go by land?'

'It would take months.'

'Juba, you just said you cared for me. And you swore! I'll go with you to Rome, but not by sea.'

'I'll think about it,' he said, after a long moment.

Abruptly, the warmth of his hand was gone and another dousing of icy foam set her teeth chattering.

He had put up the hood of his tawny cloak and was making his way unsteadily back to the captain's hut.

'Juba?' she called after him.

But he had disappeared inside the captain's hut, leaving her alone on the rain-swollen deck with only Gartha and her misery for company.

She thought things couldn't get any worse, but then the storm struck.

Chapter Thirteen
TEMPESTAS

U rsula was composing a hymn of praise, but her song turned to a scream when the lightning struck.

She had been riding the apex of the ship, swinging wildly above a glassy sea with the wind tugging her hair and rain cooling her face. Doctor Jonathan said that she liked the cold and the wet because those elements balanced the hot and dry aspects of her choleric nature.

Ursula was sorry that Bouda and Gartha had not yet found their sea legs.

She could see the two of them lying on the deck far below. She prayed they would feel better, but joy refused to let her be downcast and she began to compose a song of praise, thanking God for helping Prasutus get away.

Then the world was split by an enormous thunderclap and a stab of lightning so bright that it almost blinded her. Her ears rang, and the air was full of fizzing energy. She felt her hair standing on end. Below her on the deck, Gartha's fur was standing straight out, and Bouda's hair too. It made them both look utterly bizarre. She was about to laugh when she realised she was slowly toppling towards the sea. Lightning must have struck the mainmast and now it was falling, taking the yardarm with it.

And the sail below her was on fire!

That was when she screamed.

As the yardarm sank closer and closer to the waves, her mind raced. Should she jump into the water to escape the flames? If she did she would certainly be drowned. She could paddle in a river or stream, but not in icy waves twenty feet high. Should she jump on to the deck? No. It was still too far away and she might break her legs or, even worse, her back. Doctor Jonathan had once told her about a farmer who had been paralysed by a fall and was trapped in his unmoving body.

The others were out of the cabin now and Captain Caerulus was telling them how to put out the fire. Everyone was rushing to find buckets when a huge wave extinguished the fire in a glassy roar.

And washed one of the twins overboard.

'Raven!' she heard Castor cry and saw him run to the rail. 'Raven! Catch this rope!' But Raven was gone and Castor cried out in anguish.

Drenched and gasping, Ursula found the water was still rising to meet her as the yardarm continued its sickening descent.

Then she saw something.

Below her in the blue-grey water she saw Raven's dark head bob up out of the foam. He reached up his hand.

'Raven!' she screamed. With her feet on the top of the half-burnt sail and her left arm hooked around the polished oak yardarm, she reached down with her right hand. But she was still too far above him. And now, without a working sail or mast, the ship was twisting and turning like a dancer. Ursula heard Bouda scream as the boat tipped on one side, and she watched in wonder as her brother staggered across the bucking deck with a rope in one hand. Now he was trying to tie it around Bouda's waist. The British girl's hair had been a copper-coloured cloud a moment before but as an icy wave drenched them both, her hair covered her face like a shroud.

Then the wind spun them away and gave Ursula a new view. Beside her, a watery mountain was rising up and she could see Raven in it, held like a fly in grey-green amber. His horror-stricken eyes were level with hers and for a moment he was close enough for her to reach out and catch his hand.

But then the wave swept him away and now she was skimming above a seascape of glassy hills and valleys.

'Gartha!' screamed Ursula. As if in answer, her spar swung round and now she could see that Juba was tying a rope around Gartha too.

Two sailors were hanging on to slippery ropes, and as her part of the yardarm swung away she saw the captain swing an axe against the base of the mast. He was going to chop it down, like a tree!

Meanwhile, Castor was staggering from one side of the ship to the other, rope in hand, frantically trying to spot his brother.

For a third time the yardarm swung Ursula away and this time it plunged her right under the icy water. Her fingers were so numb that she almost let go. Then, once again, she found herself above the deck. But this time there was no sail or rope to stand on. Her feet were flailing and her frozen hands were slipping from the yardarm.

On the deck below, Juba and Doctor Jonathan were looking up at her.

'Jump now!' shouted Juba.

'I'll catch you!' cried Doctor Jonathan. Bouda lay on the deck nearby, clinging to Gartha.

It was the closest to the deck she had been. But was it close enough?

'Jump!' cried Juba again.

Once, a few months before, she had jumped from a similar height, but then she had been healthy and strong and filled with confidence. This time she was numb, cold and terrified.

'Help me, Lord!' Ursula prayed. Then she let go of the yardarm.

Jonathan's God must have heard her, for the doctor himself broke her fall.

'Ooof!' grunted Doctor Jonathan as she landed on him.

'Help!' came a voice and she saw Raven in the water, clinging to the charred remnants of the sail.

'Castor!' Ursula screamed. 'He's there! Raven is there!'

She ran to the side and started to pull in Raven's sail. A moment later Castor was beside her, and then Juba and Doctor Jonathan. Soon all hands had joined together to pull him in.

Finally Raven was back on board and the twins were embracing, sobbing in each other's arms.

Already the squall had passed and, although the ship was still bucking like a mule on coals, they were no longer in danger of sinking.

Soon it was calm enough for Captain Caerulus to light a brazier and heat a bowl of wine for them all. Doctor Jonathan added some special herbs from his big leather shoulder bag. By the time the sailors had lashed the mast to the side of the ship, Jonathan had filled their copper beakers with the steaming brew and they drank gratefully.

Then, to everyone's surprise, the sun came out, gilding the sodden timbers with its watery light. The squall was a distant blur on the horizon. The merchant ship *Centaur* was maimed but alive.

'*Carpe diem!*' cried Loquax, flying out from the cubbyhole beneath the foremast, and even Gartha gave a few feeble thumps of her tail. Ursula laughed and flopped back on the steaming deck, letting the weak sunlight warm her face.

'Land!' cried Bouda weakly. She had been at the rail being sick but now she was pointing. 'I see land!'

'Praise Venus and Neptune!' cried Captain Caerulus. 'It's the coast of Gaul!' And he barked an order to the sailors. 'Unfurl the artemon! And keep a sharp eye out for the lighthouse at Gesoriacum!'

Ursula scrambled to her feet. Within moments the small sail at the *Centaur*'s prow had filled with wind and the captain was steering them towards a smudge of blue on the horizon.

Everyone cheered. All except for poor Bouda, who was being sick again.

Ursula ran to Doctor Jonathan. He was binding up a cut on Raven's left forearm while Castor stood over them and watched.

'Doctor Jonathan! Raven! Castor!' she cried. 'We should offer thanks to God.'

'Yes, we should,' said the doctor, tying off the strip of linen and standing up.

'Let's go and stand by Gartha,' said Ursula. 'She wants to give thanks, too, but she's too weak to move.'

The twins laughed and even Jonathan gave a half smile.

They stood in a circle around Gartha and lifted their faces and hands to the sky. Castor prayed first in Hebrew and then in Latin.

'*The Lord is my rock, my fortress and my deliverer . . .*' Castor's eyes were overflowing as he spoke the next verse. '*He reached*

76

down from on high and took hold of me; he drew me out of deep waters.'

Castor could not continue so Jonathan took over. '*The Lord lives! Praise be to my Rock.*'

'*Amen!*' whispered Ursula, and Gartha thumped her tail.

Ursula hugged each of the twins and Doctor Jonathan for a long time. They hugged her back and one of the twins kissed the top of her head. She felt so full of love and gratitude that when she saw Juba standing shyly nearby she ran to hug him too.

He gave her a quick hug and then turned to the twins. 'I guess you won't be sailing on to Rome after such a narrow escape from death?'

The twins looked at each other and shrugged. 'Why not?' they said. 'God is protecting us.'

'Well, Bouda doesn't want to sail any more,' Juba said. 'So I think we should make the rest of the journey by land.'

'Wasn't that our original plan?' asked Doctor Jonathan with a frown.

Ursula nodded her agreement. 'I thought we were going to travel by road to that Colonia place where Fronto is stationed.'

'Yes, of course,' said Juba. He turned to Bouda, who was slumped miserably by the rail. 'I'll just tell Bouda the good news.'

Doctor Jonathan looked at Ursula with a puzzled frown. 'That was strange,' he murmured.

Ursula grinned. 'Those two are always strange together,' she said. 'They've been in love with each other for ages but they're both afraid to admit it.'

II

Chapter Fourteen
GESORIACUM

The scent of fresh bread and a bird's persistent chirp coaxed Bouda out of a deep sleep.

Praise the gods: she was in a dry bed and she could sense daylight beyond her closed eyelids. 'Please, Minerva, may I be on solid ground,' she whispered, clutching the gem around her neck. Then she opened her eyes to see a dim ceiling of white plaster and wooden beams.

Another whiff of bread made her stomach growl fiercely.

Bouda sat up, rubbed the sleep from her eyes and looked around a small room with white walls. Slivers of bright sunlight pushed through faded green shutters. Her cloak hung from a peg and there was another bed – an empty one – beside hers. The hastily thrown back blanket and faint whiff of dog told her that Gartha and Ursula had recently been there.

Laughter and Loquax's voice saying '*Cave Domitian!*' drifted through the slats of the shutters. She pushed back the cover and found she was barefoot but still wearing both her tunics.

The temperature of the room was fresh, but not chilly, and when she pushed the shutters open they let in a flood of golden daylight. Leaning out of the window, she saw a gravel courtyard below and her friends seated at a long table, eating and drinking, with big Gartha sitting attentively beside Ursula.

'*What ARE you doing?*' said Loquax, fluttering up to her window.

Everyone but Gartha – intent on her mistress's plate – looked up at her and waved.

'Good morning!' cried Juba. 'Come and have breakfast before we eat it all!'

Bouda quickly used the chamber pot, pulled on her boots and made her way downstairs. There she found the doorway blocked by two giggling serving girls looking into the courtyard. When she touched their shoulders they moved aside to let her through. As Bouda emerged into the bright courtyard, the crunch of gravel under her boots and the purity of light told her she was in a different land.

There were five of them, sitting both sides of a trestle table. The twins were flanking Doctor Jonathan on one bench with Juba and Ursula on the other.

'I saved you a place.' Juba patted the cushion next to him on the bench. 'You must be starving. Let me pour you a beaker of mulsum.' He looked clean and rested. As she sat on the cushion beside him, she could smell lavender body-oil. She guessed the men, at least, had been to the baths.

'Oh, it's so good to be on solid ground,' she said, and took a sip of the warm spiced wine. Her stomach growled loudly and they all laughed.

'Here!' said Ursula. 'Try this!' She passed Bouda half a buttered white roll with something translucent and orange on it. The bread was warm and the orange-coloured spread was both tart and sweet.

'What is it?' Bouda asked, still chewing. 'It's delicious.'

Ursula said, 'Quinces preserved in honey. Isn't it good?'

Bouda nodded. 'Are we in Gaul?'

Across the table, Castor laughed. 'Yes, we're in Gallia Comata, which some people call Long-haired Gaul. This part is known as Gallia Belgica. Don't you remember? The wind died just as we were nearing land but two ships came to our rescue and towed us into the Roman port.'

Raven said, 'Part of the Roman fleet is here, along with all the things we need to repair the *Centaur*.'

Castor said, 'I've just signed a deed to Juba, giving him half-ownership of the *Centaur*.'

Bouda looked at Juba in surprise. 'Why?'

'I gave him the Emerald of Smyrna,' said Juba, 'so that he could sell it to pay for repairs to the *Centaur*. And also so that we can offer a sheep as thanks to the gods for a safe landfall. We're going to the temple of Neptune soon. We were just waiting for you to get up.'

Bouda put down her half-eaten roll and said firmly, 'You can offer a dozen sheep to a dozen gods but I'll never set foot on another ship.'

Juba smiled. 'You don't have to,' he said. 'Castor and Raven plan to sail on to Ostia but we're going to travel by land.'

Bouda stared at the twins. 'You're going to go back on a ship after what happened?'

Castor and Raven looked at each other and shrugged. 'My brother's God saved me,' said Raven. 'If he did it once he can do it again.'

'Storms at sea, robbers by land,' said Doctor Jonathan as he spread quince preserve on his freshly buttered roll. 'Disaster will find you no matter how you travel.'

They all made the sign against evil, even Bouda.

Ursula gave the doctor an affectionate thump on the arm.

'Don't be such a pessimist,' she said. 'We have Gartha to protect us against robbers!'

'I can't help being a pessimist,' said Doctor Jonathan with grim satisfaction. 'My temperament is melancholic. Too much black bile.'

'What happened to Prasutus?' asked Bouda. 'I was too sick to take notice of anything.'

'Tortor was about to prod him with a red-hot poker and make him betray us,' said Ursula.

'But he got away,' said Juba.

'He did the backflip Caudex taught us,' said Castor.

'It was beautiful,' added Raven. 'He brought down two soldiers, that fat Roman and the torturer. Caudex would have been proud.'

Ursula put down her unfinished roll. 'But that means we'll probably never see Prasutus again,' she said with a sigh.

'Or the torturer, either,' said Juba.

'I wouldn't be so sure,' said Doctor Jonathan. 'Tortor's job is to hunt down opponents of the Emperor. We should go as soon as we can.'

'*Go as soon as we can,*' echoed Loquax.

Bouda started to rise from her seat. 'Now?'

Juba shook his head. 'We think one good thing about that squall is that it bought us an extra few days at least. Our pursuers will have no idea where we are, or even if we survived.'

'Even so,' said Doctor Jonathan, 'we should go as soon as possible.'

'Captain Caerulus is down at the docks overseeing repairs to the *Centaur*,' said Castor. 'With any luck Raven and I will set sail at dawn tomorrow.'

'If Doctor Jonathan allows us to stay another half a day,' said Juba, 'then we can leave at dawn too.'

The doctor gave a grudging nod.

Juba smiled at Bouda. 'That means you and Ursula can visit the baths. There's a small public bath-house down the road.'

'Praise Minerva!' breathed Bouda. 'Do any of you have a strigil we can borrow? And oil?'

'You can use my strigil,' said Doctor Jonathan.

Juba gave Bouda a sestertius. 'They sell measures of scented olive oil for a quadrans each. That should be enough.'

An hour later, relaxed and sweaty, Bouda sat on a warm marble bench in the women's section of a small but clean bath-house and let Ursula scrape lavender-scented oil from her back.

'Bouda?' said Ursula.

'Yes?' Bouda kept her eyes closed, luxuriating in the feel of the dull bronze blade of the strigil on her oily skin.

'Will you miss Britannia?'

'No. There's nothing for me there. In Londinium my only family was a gang of cutpurses and none of us trusted the other. I didn't really feel at home in the Belgae village either. But I liked living in Caudex's villa, apart from hiding every time someone made a delivery.'

Ursula stopped scraping. 'Bouda,' she said, 'what is your heart's desire?'

'What do you mean?'

'My heart's desire is to help animals.' Ursula continued scraping. 'And maybe be an animal doctor. If I had a signet ring like yours I would ask the gem carver to put a horse, a dog and a bird on it. Juba's desire is to be good, so he might have Aeneas on his ring. What would you put on your ring?'

'I'm not sure. I want lots of things.'

But later, when Bouda lay back on the bench, closed her eyes and thought about Ursula's question, an image arose in her mind's eye.

She saw a green inner garden with curved marble benches and a splashing fountain and a statue of Minerva at its centre. It was like the inner garden of Caudex's villa and yet it was different.

Did it mean they had made a mistake in leaving the protection that Caudex offered? Or something else?

Chapter Fifteen
TINCTA

The next morning before dawn, Ursula and the others packed their few belongings and went to the harbour. The Roman port of Gesoriacum was on their way to Colonia and they wanted to make sure Castor and Raven got away safely. A few flickering torches showed early activity in the harbour, so they hung back in the shadows, not wanting to attract the attention of any soldiers or guards. Ursula waited for the others to say goodbye to the twins before stepping forward. 'Look after Loquax?' She handed one of the twins the covered birdcage. 'I don't want anyone to be hurt or killed because of something I trained him to say.'

The twin nodded and took the cage. He wore his grey cloak with the hood up, and she could hardly see his face.

She could only tell it was Raven when he spoke. 'On board a ship,' he whispered, 'nobody will hear Loquax telling us to beware of Domitian. We'll look after him.'

Ursula gave a brave smile. 'Thank you.'

Beside him, Castor leaned forward and whispered, 'Captain Caerulus says Loquax is the reason we didn't sink. He says the bird has Fortuna's favour.'

Ursula nodded. 'Farewell. Maybe one day I'll see you in Rome . . .'

'Ostia,' corrected Castor. 'It's fifteen miles from Rome.'

'I'll see you in Ostia,' said Ursula. 'God willing.'

Without any apparent signal or prior agreement, Castor and Raven both bent forward. Castor kissed Ursula's left cheek and Raven her right. She could feel the beginnings of their beards and she was overwhelmed by a sudden surge of love for them. This love was not like her previous infatuation with the twins. It was a holy love, the love of God flowing through her.

'Dear Lord,' she whispered, 'protect Castor and Raven and Loquax, and the rest of the crew aboard the *Centaur*.'

'*Amen*,' they murmured in unison, and pulled back. Although it was still dark she could see tears gleaming in their eyes.

'Take care of Loquax,' she whispered as the twins turned to go. 'Don't feed him too many raisins or he gets diarrhoea.'

The twins gave identical laughs and headed towards the *Centaur*. As the others waved, Ursula knelt down, put her arms around Gartha and buried her face in her dog's woolly neck. All these farewells were so painful. She could hardly bear to watch.

But when she heard deep male voices she raised her head and stood up, heart pounding. Two soldiers holding torches had stopped the twins at the foot of the gangplank.

Ursula's heart skipped a beat when a flickering torchlight showed one of the soldiers lifting the cover of Loquax's cage.

There was a pause and then a faint, '*What ARE you doing?*' from Loquax.

The soldiers cursed and then laughed. She heard one wishing them a good voyage as they moved away.

Ursula breathed a prayer of relief as the sailors untied the ship and began to pull up the gangplank. *Praise God Loquax hadn't mentioned the Emperor.*

A lamp swung from the curved neck of the swan's head at the

stern as it started to move. Two of the sailors were using poles to push the *Centaur* away from the dock. Ursula heard the clink of tackle and the soft plop of the rudder paddles as Captain Caerulus steered the ship out into the breeze. The repaired mast stood straight and black against the grey sky of dawn. It looked like a moving tree leaving a winter forest of bare trunks. The sky was growing lighter and the world was becoming tinted with colour. The last they saw of the *Centaur* was the small disc of its lookout platform, lit golden by the rising sun.

'Come on,' said Juba, turning away. 'We'd better go before it gets light enough for someone to recognise us. Put your hood up, Ursula.'

Obediently, she put up her hood and turned to follow him.

'Doctor Jonathan,' Ursula said, 'what if Montanus and Tortor find the inn where we stayed?'

'We told the innkeeper we're heading south towards Lutetia,' said the doctor. 'But look!' He pointed. 'The sun is rising right in front of us. That means we're going which direction?'

'East,' said Ursula. 'To see Fronto. Where is he stationed again?'

'Colonia something,' said Bouda.

'Yes,' said Juba. 'Colonia Claudia Ara Agrippinensium in full. Claudius named it after his wife Agrippina, who was born there,' he added, 'so that she would be remembered for all time.'

After a moment Bouda said, 'I'll always remember Agrippina for being murdered by her son, Nero.'

Ursula shuddered but she saw Juba give Bouda an approving look; before their flight from Britannia, he had been teaching them about the emperors of Rome.

By now they had left the warehouses of the port and were moving along a wide street near the potters' market towards the east gate. It was still early but people were already about. Some of the townspeople were fair, but most of them had dark hair and eyes. Almost every man had long hair, in keeping with the nickname of the province: Long-haired Gaul.

Ursula had an uneasy feeling. Something felt wrong.

Had she left something behind?

She realised it was the absence of weight on her shoulders. Usually Meer sat on her left shoulder or curled around her neck while Loquax chattered on her right shoulder. It was as if part of her was gone. She took a deep breath and blinked back tears. She must be brave.

Thank goodness she had faithful Gartha trotting beside her. She patted her dog's big head and Gartha panted happily.

'Look at the yarn!' Bouda pointed up. 'Isn't it beautiful?'

They were entering the dyers' market, where stalls were already open. Up above them, hanging skeins of cloth and wool were now lit by the newly risen sun as it shone through the open eastern gate of the town.

'Those loops of yarn look like jewelled necklaces,' said Bouda.

They stopped and looked up.

'Jasper, sapphire, chrysolite and topaz,' said Doctor Jonathan.

'I think it's a good omen,' said Juba. 'The sun probably only shines through this gate a few times a year.'

'We should disguise ourselves!' Ursula said suddenly. 'I could cut off my hair and pretend to be a boy like Juba.'

Doctor Jonathan groaned. 'You sound just like your patroness, Flavia Gemina. She and her freedwoman Nubia used to disguise themselves as boys,' he said.

Ursula clutched his free arm, the one without the staff. 'Juba and I could be your dark-skinned slave-boys from Africa. Bouda's too curvy to be a boy so she could be your wife.'

'It might work,' Jonathan said. 'But there's one member of our party who can't be disguised.' He raised his eyebrows at Gartha and resumed walking towards the gate again.

Ursula ran to catch up. 'We could put long ears on her and hitch her to a raeda and pretend she's a donkey.'

Doctor Jonathan gave a bark of laughter. Then his smile faded and he stopped dead in his tracks.

'Tigris!' he cried, his eyes wide. 'Tiger!'

Chapter Sixteen
FLOCCI

The blood leapt in Juba's veins when the doctor cried, 'Tiger!'

'Where?' He stepped closer to Bouda and unsheathed his dagger. 'Where's the tiger?'

'In Ostia.' Doctor Jonathan gave a sheepish grin. 'Back in Ostia, many years ago. Tigris was my pet.'

'You had a pet tiger?' gasped Ursula.

The doctor shook his head. 'No, it was the name of a dog I had when I was a boy. We called him Tigris after a creature mentioned by Pliny, the naturalist. It's a cross between a dog and a tiger.'

Bouda raised an eyebrow at the dagger in Juba's hand so he quickly put it away. He scowled at the doctor. 'How does that help us?'

'I know!' cried Ursula. 'We can paint stripes on Gartha and pretend she's a tiger-dog!'

Doctor Jonathan grinned. 'I was thinking of a lion-dog.'

'Oh yes!' cried Ursula, clapping her hands.

'Nobody will be fooled by that,' muttered Juba.

'That doesn't matter,' said the doctor. 'It's a distraction. People won't be talking about the two dusky-skinned children and the girl with flaming red hair. They'll be talking about the travelling doctor and his lion-dog.'

Juba glanced at Bouda. She gave him a little smile and a one-shouldered shrug, as if to say *why not?*

'We can give her a mane!' Ursula was almost jumping up and down with excitement.

Juba sighed. 'But where would we get the material?'

'There.' Bouda was pointing at some coloured skeins of wool hanging above them. 'I left most of my sewing and weaving things in Britannia but one of my bone hairpins is also a needle.' She reached up under her leaf-green palla and pulled it out of the tight knot of copper-coloured hair at the back of her head. 'See? It's got quite a wide eye. I can easily stitch woolly clumps of wool to a band of felt and we can tie it around Gartha's head.'

Juba raised an eyebrow. 'How do you know what a lion looks like? They don't have them in Britannia.'

'A signifer at the legionary fortress last year,' Bouda replied. 'He wore a lion skin.'

'I remember!' cried Ursula. 'That mane was tawny yellow but I'm sure you can get brown manes.' She looked at the doctor. 'You were in the arena with a lion, weren't you? Flavia Gemina told us the story and Lupus acted it out once in a pantomime.'

'It's true,' said Doctor Jonathan. 'I once faced a lion in Rome's new amphitheatre. His name was Monobaz. I don't think it matters what colour the mane is,' he added.

'I think it's a foolish idea,' said Juba.

Doctor Jonathan put a hand on Juba's arm. 'It's worth a try,' he said. Then he turned to Bouda. 'Choose what you need,' he said. 'I'll pay for the wool.'

As Bouda was haggling with the stall-keeper in a language like Brittonic, the doctor said to Juba, 'When I enter a new town

I usually tie my bleeding-cup to the top of my staff to let people know I'm a doctor. But sometimes people don't notice me. This way I'll be sure to get attention.'

Juba did not meet the doctor's gaze but kept his eyes on Bouda. He did not entirely like Doctor Jonathan or the hold he had over his little sister. He was especially uneasy about the doctor's strange religion. It had made Ursula even more gullible than she had been before.

'It's also not a bad idea,' said the doctor, 'that Bouda pretends to be my wife and you and Ursula pose as my slaves.'

Juba's head whipped around and he glared at the doctor.

'Whoa!' said Doctor Jonathan, putting up both hands. 'It's only for show. We can try it out to see if it works.'

'I've got the mane!' Bouda came up with a smile and a large clump of brown wool. Her smile faded when she saw their expressions. 'What's the matter?'

'Ursula and I have been demoted to slaves,' said Juba through gritted teeth. 'And you are now the doctor's wife.'

Bouda laughed. 'It's only pretend.'

Juba turned his head away so she wouldn't see the emotions on his face.

'Doctor Jonathan,' said Bouda, 'how old are you?'

'Old!' The doctor sighed as they turned to follow Ursula, who was being tugged towards the town gate by Gartha. 'I'll be twenty-eight next September.'

Bouda pushed a stray tendril of copper hair back under her palla. 'Why aren't you married?'

The doctor sighed. 'I was too busy searching for Castor's brother,' he said.

'But now that the twins are reunited you can look for a wife.'

'I suppose.'

Bouda glanced at Juba. 'Isn't it true that Roman men sometimes marry girls much younger than themselves?'

Juba realised his fists were clenching. He took a deep breath and let it out slowly. He knew Bouda was teasing him and it made him angry.

'Oh yes,' Doctor Jonathan said. 'Men of forty or even fifty often marry girls your age.'

Bouda took the doctor's free arm. 'So it's totally believable that I could be your wife, isn't it? You're only fourteen years older than I am.' She gave Juba a laughing glance over her shoulder.

Juba felt sick.

Then he remembered the words of Seneca: *Those whom the gods love, they test.*

This is just a test, Juba, to make you strong, he told himself. *You've got a two-thousand-mile journey ahead. Go along with their plan. Be a slave. After all, even Seneca tried living life in poverty once.*

Chapter Seventeen
COMAE

As Doctor Jonathan used his sharpest scalpel to chop off Ursula's hair, she watched Bouda make a lion's mane for Gartha. Sitting in the shade of a friendly oak, they had eaten a late lunch of cold mutton left over from the previous day's sacrifice. Now they were transforming themselves.

Bouda worked quickly, using her bone hairpin-needle to sew clumps of dark brown wool on to a band of felt. The doctor was quick, too, and Ursula felt the weight of her long black curls fall away. She didn't mind. It felt wonderful to have a light cool head.

'All done,' said the doctor, showing Ursula two handfuls of her silky black hair. She barely looked at it, for Bouda had just finished. With a cry of delight, Ursula snatched Gartha's mane from Bouda's hands and knelt to tie it around her dog's head.

Then she stood back and gave it an appraising look.

'Great Jupiter's eyebrows!' exclaimed Juba as he emerged from some nearby bushes. 'You look like a boy, Ursula. A pretty boy, but still a boy. And Gartha looks like a furry sphinx!'

'That's because she's sitting down,' said Ursula. 'Come on, Gartha!' she called. 'Up you get! Time to go!'

With a sigh, Gartha heaved herself to her feet. It occurred

to Ursula, not for the first time, that her beloved hound was getting old.

'She looks rather doleful,' observed the doctor. 'I don't think she'll frighten anybody.'

But he was proved wrong a quarter of an hour later when the sight of Gartha wearing her woollen lion's mane sent two little girls screaming back towards their settlement. The children's squeals brought the locals out of their houses and in from the fields.

Most kept their distance, staring wide-eyed, but a few brandished axes or heavy walking sticks as they moved closer.

Ursula quickly knelt and patted Gartha to show that she was not a threat.

Everyone gasped.

Then some of the bolder boys came forward to stroke her, too, followed by the little girls, who touched Gartha and then jumped back laughing. Soon people realised that the lion was just a big scent-hound wearing a mane, but Gartha had done her job: she had attracted their attention. When people saw the bronze bleeding-cup tied to the end of Jonathan's staff, they realised he was a doctor and eagerly came forward with their ailments.

Now almost all of them wanted to touch the lion-dog, whom they regarded as a good luck talisman. Gartha sat patiently, panting with her big pink tongue. After everyone had finished stroking her, Ursula gave her a rind of yellow cheese as a treat.

At that first village, a rich landowner asked Jonathan to treat his sick wife. When Jonathan prescribed a day of fasting and steam baths followed by a change in diet, the man offered them bed and board in his Roman-style villa so that Jonathan could oversee the treatment.

When the man showed them to a room with a feather bed for the 'married couple' but only two rush mats on the floor for their 'slaves', Ursula had to bite her lip to keep from laughing at the expression of outrage on Juba's face.

Of course, Jonathan took one of the mats and let Ursula and Bouda share the feather bed with Gartha, but Juba was still sulky.

Two days later the man's wife was much improved and they were on their way.

That afternoon Jonathan set the broken leg of a Roman glassmaker who lived with his German wife in a roundhouse like the ones they had known in Britannia. While Juba assisted with the splint, Ursula prepared a poultice. But Bouda was encouraged to sit in the family's best wicker chair with a bowl of raisins and a glass of honeyed wine on a table beside her. The glassmaker and his wife had no slaves, but their eleven-year-old daughter, Januaria Lepida, came to arrange Bouda's hair in a combination of plaits and tendrils.

'You have beautiful hair,' Ursula heard the daughter tell Bouda. 'It's so distinctive.'

'I like your hair, too,' said Bouda. 'It's such a pretty colour, like honey.'

Suddenly, before Januaria could finish plaiting her hair, Bouda stood up and whispered something in the girl's ear. Januaria nodded and they both went out of the roundhouse.

Two hours later Bouda returned with her beautiful copper hair a dull brown.

Gartha wagged her tail but Ursula cried, 'Bouda! What have you done?'

'Be quiet, impudent slave!' Bouda gave her a stern look.

Ursula bit her lip to keep from giggling; she kept forgetting the role she was supposed to be playing.

Later, in their screened-off part of the roundhouse, Bouda examined her hair in the light of a candle. 'Januaria dyed it with walnut and iron scrapings on my request,' she whispered, 'so that I won't look so distinctive. Does it make me very ugly?' she asked Juba, who was staring at her in dismay.

'No, not at all,' he stammered. 'It just makes you look different . . .' Then he trailed off in confusion.

And so it continued. They would walk for a few days, then stay with someone who needed healing.

Sometimes they were paid in coin, but more often in goods.

In one village, a cobbler paid them with repairs to their shoes and a new pair of butter-soft slippers for 'the doctor's wife'. In another settlement, a cloth merchant gave them a bolt of tartan wool in shades of apricot and green, an extremely valuable gift. Bouda sewed herself a new tunic and gave Ursula her old tartan one. Ursula didn't mind. Bouda loved beautiful things, but Ursula had never cared about what she wore.

A cheerful farmer gave them a new skin full of sweet white wine. 'Will you hold the wine?' Jonathan asked Ursula. 'And don't let me have more than a few squirts in my cup. Wine is my weakness.'

'Then why keep it?' asked Ursula.

Doctor Jonathan shrugged. 'It's useful for medicinal purposes.'

'Better give it to me, then,' said Juba.

The best gift, in Ursula's opinion, was a little glass phial full of pale yellow liquid.

The huntsman who gave it to them called it 'essence of wolf'.

'Put this on your lion-dog,' he said, 'and she'll scare the village dogs as well as the inhabitants. But wait until after you've left my hut,' he added quickly as Ursula started to pull out the little cork. 'Or my own dogs will run for the hills.'

Everywhere they were fed and watered and given a safe place to sleep.

The people of this region loved sausage and pickled cabbage and brown rye bread. Poplar trees lined the road and wildflowers dotted the verge.

Three days before the end of April, rejoicing villagers gave them flowered garlands to wear in honour of the Floralia and told them that Colonia was about two hundred miles distant. If they averaged ten miles a day they could reach it by the third week of May.

That night, Ursula assisted Jonathan at the birth of a child. When she heard the first wail of a newborn, the sound brought tears to her eyes and a deep sense of joy. She and Jonathan always whispered prayers over those they treated, both human and animal. This time they also sang a soft song of praise, thanking God for new birth.

And so they moved on steadily, with the sun in their eyes every morning and warming their backs every evening.

So far they had not had any sense of being followed by a masked man in black robes or anyone else. Their ruse of travelling as a doctor, his wife, two slaves and a lucky lion-dog seemed to be working.

Little did Ursula dream what awaited them on the road ahead.

Chapter Eighteen
MORS

As they proceeded east to Colonia, Juba found his thoughts returning again and again to baby Dora in Ostia. If they only knew the date on which Domitian was fated to die, they could aim to arrive in Rome's port soon after. With the Emperor out of the way, they could safely visit baby Dora and the family who had adopted her.

Juba decided to make Doctor Jonathan tell him the date of the tyrant's predicted demise.

His first approach was to challenge Jonathan's sense of justice.

'Aren't you angry about what Remus is doing?' he asked the doctor on the Kalends of May. Remus was their code name for Domitian because Remus was the lesser brother of Rome's founder Romulus, and Domitian was the younger brother of the Emperor Titus.

'I hate what Remus is doing,' said Jonathan. 'He kept me prisoner when I was your age and tortured me for days. His brother, "Romulus", gave me this brand on my arm. But I'm not going to help you assassinate him.'

'I don't want to kill him,' said Juba. 'I just want to know when it's safe to return.'

'Even if Remus should die on the appointed day,' said

Jonathan, 'who is to say his successor will be any better? Remember, a bad ruler can be followed by an even worse one.'

A few days later Juba tried a different approach. 'Doctor Jonathan, do you believe horoscopes are accurate?'

'The holy scriptures warn us against vain attempts to predict the future,' replied the doctor.

Juba was surprised for a moment, then said, 'So they're not accurate?'

'They might be or they might not be.'

'But you told Ursula that Domitian – I mean Remus – believes his horoscope . . .'

'Yes. That is why such things are dangerous. They influence weak-minded folk, and not usually for the good.'

A week later, on the Nones of May, Juba tried a direct approach. 'Doctor Jonathan,' he said, 'as we're going to Colonia and not Rome, can you tell us the hour of Remus's prophesied death?'

To which Doctor Jonathan did not even reply.

But two days after the Ides of May, Juba finally got the doctor to reveal the fatal date.

In a village about fifty miles from Colonia, Doctor Jonathan lost a patient.

A miller's nine-year-old son had fallen from a wagon on to the merciless paving stones of the Roman road. The boy's head was swelling and Doctor Jonathan said he would certainly die if left untreated. However, there was a small chance of survival. If he could remove a coin-sized piece of the boy's skull to relieve the pressure, then the boy might live.

The doctor took out a bronze tube with tiny saw-like teeth on one end. 'I must remove a circle of bone from his head. It will be painful but it should give him relief. Ursula and Juba assisted, and the boy's screams were pathetic to hear. Jonathan worked grimly with clenched jaw and managed to remove the bone. But it was either too much or too late.

When the boy died, Doctor Jonathan wept. It was the first time Ursula had seen one of their patients die and she wept too.

They left the village quickly, almost furtively, followed by the boy's funeral procession.

That evening they camped in a clearing by the river. Juba took Gartha into the woods to hunt but they found nothing and he returned to a dinner of leathery bread and hard cheese.

It was growing dark, and there was a chill in the air, so Juba started a fire. He gathered a pile of seed fluff and small dried leaves for tinder. Nearby were twigs and larger branches that the girls had collected.

Juba took out his fire-box. It contained several pieces of what he called horse-hoof fungus. It did not come from a horse's hoof, but the growth on the tree looked like one, hence the name. When treated, this fungus was the best material for catching a spark and making it grow.

Juba struck the flint against his small square of iron. A red spark jumped on to the horse-hoof fungus and grew.

'Juba,' said Doctor Jonathan, his eyes still swollen from weeping. 'Remember I gave you a wineskin last week and told you not to give it to me?'

'Of course I remember.' Juba blew gently on the tinder; it had just caught fire.

'I want you to give it to me,' said the doctor.

'Are you sure?' said Juba, carefully placing a few twigs on the baby fire in order to build it up.

'Yes,' said the doctor. 'I have to make a potion.'

Juba frowned as he added larger twigs. 'Why don't you give me the beaker and I'll pour in what you need.'

'Very well,' said Jonathan, and extended the copper beaker they all shared. 'A quarter full.'

The wineskin was on a strap across Juba's torso. He took it off and squirted wine into the beaker.

'Ursula,' said Doctor Jonathan, 'get the poppy-tears from my bag?'

Ursula brought out the phial of milky liquid in a glass bottle shaped like a poppy head.

The three of them watched as Jonathan added three milky drops of poppy-tears, then topped up the cup with water and warmed it over Juba's now crackling fire.

Before Juba could protest, the doctor took the beaker of potion and drained it.

'Doctor Jonathan!' cried Ursula. 'That's too much!'

Sensing Ursula's distress, Gartha whined softly.

The doctor glowered at them. 'I can take it,' he said. And to Juba's astonishment he held out the empty cup. 'More wine,' he commanded. 'Fill it half full.'

'No,' said Juba. 'You told me not to give it to you. Now I know why.'

'Doctor Jonathan,' said Ursula. 'Why do you want to drink more? It's very strong!'

'I want to forget,' he said, resting his curly head in his hands.

'But you did the best you could,' Bouda protested. 'You warned the boy's parents he might die.'

'It's not just that boy I'm trying to forget.' The doctor's words were already slurred. 'It's all of them. All eighty thousand.'

'Eighty thousand what?' asked Juba, puzzled.

'Give me the wine skin and I'll tell you.'

'Oh!' cried Bouda. 'He means the people who died in the fire he started in Rome. Remember, Flavia told us the story?'

'That's right,' said Juba. 'I remember.'

'God forgave you for that,' Ursula said to Jonathan.

'Maybe I didn't forgive myself. Give me the skin!' Doctor Jonathan lunged for the wineskin but Juba easily moved it out of his reach. The doctor was already drunk on a combination of wine and poppy-tears.

'Please?' The doctor was pleading now. 'Please give me the wineskin?'

Suddenly Juba had an idea. 'Tell me the day and time,' he said. 'And I'll give you the wineskin.'

'No, Juba!' cried Ursula. 'You promised not to give him any more!'

'I also made promises to our mother before she died,' Juba said bitterly. 'And to Flavia Gemina. I've broken plenty of those.'

He turned to the doctor who was still making groggy swipes with his right hand. 'Tell me the day and the hour of the tyrant's death . . . and the wineskin is yours.'

'Thirteen days before the Kalends of October,' slurred Jonathan, 'at the fifth hour. Death by seven stab wounds, or so says Ascel . . . Asci . . . So says the soothsayer. Now give me my wine!'

Juba handed over the wineskin and watched with a mixture of pity and scorn as the doctor drained it dry. Soon Doctor Jonathan was snoring in the grass.

That night Juba's mind raced. The fateful day was mid-September, four months distant. On the one hand, that was bad, because at the pace they were going, Domitian would still be alive when they reached Ostia. On the other hand it was good because it meant that by mid-autumn they might have a

105

new Emperor. The third most terrible option was that the date was not a true prophesy but just a guess, and that the Emperor would live many more years. Or even decades.

Juba shuddered at the thought.

The next morning he braced himself for a confrontation with the doctor, but Jonathan was suffering a bad headache and could remember nothing of the night before.

'Did I say or do anything disgraceful?' he asked them as they packed up their meagre belongings.

'You vomited by that ash tree,' said Juba quickly. 'And you snored all night.'

'Nothing else?' groaned the doctor.

'Nothing,' said Juba quickly with a warning look to the girls.

They glared back at Juba, but they did not tell the doctor that he had blurted out his precious secret.

Now Juba had the information he had so desperately wanted, but no idea how use it.

Chapter Nineteen
MONILE

The thing Bouda feared most occurred a week later when they were less than twenty miles from Colonia. They had just left the villa of a retired centurion named Celerinus, who owned a large estate. Doctor Jonathan had cured the centurion's sick wife with a most unusual treatment. He had commanded a female donkey be brought into the sickroom and had made Celerinus's wife drink milk straight from the donkey's udder.

Celerinus paid them in silver and they had been on the road about an hour when they heard the sound of baying dogs, and looked at each other in alarm.

'Do you think those dogs are after us?' asked Ursula.

'Tortor!' cried Juba.

'Maybe,' said Doctor Jonathan. 'Or maybe not. In case they are after us, remember to play your roles. We've been getting lazy. Ursula, put a few drops of that wolf essence on Gartha.'

'Good idea!' cried Ursula.

Bouda could smell the hot stink of wolf as Ursula dribbled two drops on to the back of her dog's neck. Gartha didn't like it, but she was used to the smell of wolf from her days in the arena and they had used the essence twice before to keep away fierce village dogs. Ursula was just replacing the cork on the phial when the baying hounds crested the rise and came running towards them.

There were three of them, ugly creatures with flat faces and spikes on their collars, but the moment they caught Gartha's wolfy scent, they ran yelping into the woods.

Their owner wasn't as easily fooled.

It was the ex-centurion Celerinus, followed by two big slaves carrying a sella, a chair on poles covered by curtains. Bouda noticed he was wearing a sword.

'Halt!' he bellowed in his training-ground voice. He pointed a meaty forefinger at them. 'I want a word with you!'

Bouda and the others stopped.

'Dear Lord,' muttered Jonathan. 'Don't tell me his wife died.' And in a louder voice he said, 'Greetings, sir. I hope your wife has not taken a turn for the worse?'

'My wife's health is fine,' shouted Celerinus, 'but she is in tears because her favourite necklace is missing and she thinks someone stole it!'

Bouda's heart sank, but Juba laughed.

The man turned on him with a furious red face. 'WHY ARE YOU LAUGHING?' he bellowed in a voice as loud as any town crier's.

'I'm sorry, sir,' said Juba. 'We're just relieved. We thought it was something more serious.'

'But this *is* serious! My wife's necklace is gone. A beautiful necklace of gold, emerald and amethyst. It used to belong to her mother and her mother's mother. It was her dowry,' he added.

'We're sorry your wife lost her necklace,' said Doctor Jonathan politely, 'but we promise you we don't have it.'

'Then you won't mind me searching you,' he said.

Although it was not a question, Doctor Jonathan bowed. 'Of course not,' he said, and held out his arms.

The ex-centurion snapped his fingers at one of the sella-carriers, a big male slave with a missing front tooth. The gap-toothed slave patted Doctor Jonathan all over, then started to tip the contents of his leather satchel on to the road.

'Hey!' cried the doctor. 'I have valuable equipment in there. If you must take them out, put them on this.' He put down his walking stick, removed his cloak and spread it on the road. Then he himself took out his instruments one by one. 'This is my capsa.' He took off the top of a felt-lined metal cylinder and held it up so Celerinus could see. 'It contains my probes, hooks, tweezers and spoons.' He replaced the lid of the capsa and began to bring out other items. 'Catheter, speculum, bone drill, skull saw, strigil. This, of course, is a bleeding-cup. And these are my forceps. Those little cloth bags are for herbs – you don't have to open them, just feel them – and this is the mortar and pestle I use to grind them. This bottle holds poppy-tears and this one has oil for the baths.'

'Those two scrolls?' asked Celerinus.

'One on how to live, one on medicine.'

'No. I mean open them up.'

'You have only to look at them to see there is nothing hidden in them.'

'Very well. What's in the leather wallet?'

'My surgery tools.'

As the doctor unfolded a large leather wallet containing a dozen sharp scalpels, each in its own section, Bouda felt queasy. Not because of what she saw, but because they might want to search her too.

Jonathan showed the now empty satchel to the gap-toothed

109

slave, who peered into its depths, then shook his head at his master.

'What about your slave-boys?' growled Celerinus. 'Maybe one of them took it.'

Doctor Jonathan nodded at Juba and Ursula. Juba's jaw clenched at this indignity, but he held out his arms. After a pat-down, Gap-Tooth examined his belt, knife, waterskin and fire-box. Finally he reached down the front of Juba's tunic and pulled out the little bronze Mercury, a napkin and a hunting sling.

When Gap-Tooth moved on to Ursula, big Gartha growled deep in her throat.

'It's all right, Gartha,' said Ursula, and she submitted to the search. She kept her face blank as Gap-Tooth fished down the front of her tunic. Bouda knew Ursula was still flat as a plank. Hopefully he wouldn't suspect she was a girl.

The slave extracted a folding spoon, a napkin and the stubby end of a sausage. The sight of this made Gartha wag her tail.

Gap-Tooth finished searching Ursula as Doctor Jonathan was putting the last of his instruments back in his satchel. The doctor stood up and spread his hands. 'See?' he said. 'We are innocent of any theft.'

By now a small crowd had gathered on the bright road to see what was happening.

'What about your wife?' Celerinus suddenly pointed at Bouda. 'If she really is your wife. My slaves said you sleep on the floor with one of your slaves and the younger slave beds down with her.'

Bouda's heart was beating so hard she thought she might be sick.

'I don't have it,' she protested, but it came out as a whisper.

She tried to swallow but her throat was dry. 'Please, no!' she said in a louder voice. She saw Juba step forward to protect her but a warning glance from Jonathan reminded him that he was supposed to be a slave.

Instead, Doctor Jonathan came to stand beside her. 'My wife is beyond reproach,' he said, putting his arm awkwardly around her shoulders. Then he brought his arm away as if he had been burnt, and stared at her. She knew then that he had felt her trembling violently; he must have guessed the truth.

Doctor Jonathan quickly recovered himself. 'I refuse to let a common slave touch one hairpin on my wife's head or even the sole of her sandal.'

'Then I will do it!' A woman pulled back the covering of the sella and stepped out on to the road. It was the centurion's wife, the patient Jonathan had cured. Her face was pale and her eyes red-rimmed from weeping. 'I'm a woman of equal status. I will search her.'

For a moment Bouda considered making a dash for freedom. But the dogs were back, hackles up and pacing uneasily behind their master. If she fled they would certainly bring her down and pluck out her throat. Unlike Gartha, she was not protected by essence of wolf.

As Celerinus's wife began to pat her all over, Bouda felt hot blood rise to her chest, throat and cheeks.

By the time the woman reached down into the neck of her tunic and triumphantly fished out the stolen necklace, Bouda knew her face was red with shame.

Chapter Twenty
TURPITUDO

When the woman pulled her glittering necklace from Bouda's tunic, Juba could not believe his eyes.

'I KNEW IT!' bellowed Celerinus, his face almost as red as Bouda's. 'You are common thieves!' He stepped forward. 'I demand that you punish her!' he cried. 'Strip her! Give her a public flogging! That will teach her!'

'Wait!' The wife was still fishing down the front of Bouda's tunic. 'There's more!' She pulled out a small ivory comb that Juba had never seen before. Then a gold coin. When had Bouda received an aureus? Finally, she grasped the Minerva gem and tried to pull it from Bouda's neck. 'I'll wager this isn't yours either!'

Juba opened his mouth, then shut it again. He was pretending to be a slave, and there was nothing he could do to help her without exposing their deception.

Doctor Jonathan stared for a moment in disbelief, then recovered his wits. 'Those things are all ours,' he lied. 'They are all gifts from me to my wife.'

The woman stopped tugging and narrowed her eyes at the objects lying on the palm of her hand. 'These are yours?' she asked, holding the comb and coin.

'Yes.' Doctor Jonathan reached out and took the comb from the woman's hand. 'This' – he held up the comb – 'used to belong to my mother. It has sentimental value. However' – he closed the woman's fingers around the gold coin – 'my wife would like to give you the aureus as an apology for the distress she caused you.' He stepped forward and spoke to the woman in a low voice. 'A demon sometimes possesses her and makes her steal things while she is still asleep. I promise I will deal with it. But please, no public beatings.'

The woman opened her fingers and looked first at the coin, then at her husband. 'May I keep it?' she asked him.

Celerinus scowled at Bouda and then at Doctor Jonathan. Behind him the dogs were growling and getting bolder. 'Do you promise you will punish her?'

'I promise,' said Doctor Jonathan.

Celerinus turned to his wife. 'Are you sure? Wouldn't you rather see her beaten?'

'I'm sure, Marcus,' she said. 'I'm feeling tired now. Please take me home?'

'Very well.' Celerinus helped his wife back into her sella and turned to Doctor Jonathan. 'If I hear of anything like this happening again, I swear I will take my dogs and hunt you down and have you ALL stripped and flogged!'

'Yes, sir.' Jonathan bowed his head. Juba and Ursula followed suit and so did Bouda, gazing miserably at the paving-stones of the Roman road.

When the centurion and his wife and the onlookers had gone, the four of them turned and walked in silence for a short time. Juba felt sick with disappointment. Once again, his hopes that Bouda had changed had been destroyed.

When at last they crested a rise and found the road ahead

empty, he rounded on Bouda. 'How long have you been stealing?'

Bouda dropped her head, letting her dyed brown hair hide her face.

'Bouda!' he said sharply.

Her sulky expression almost made her look plain.

'All my life,' she muttered. 'I've been stealing all my life. It's what I do.'

'The coin and comb didn't belong to the centurion's wife,' said Doctor Jonathan. 'So where did you get them? We'll have to replace the coin and return the comb.'

'What?' cried Ursula. 'Go all the way back to wherever she stole them from?'

Gartha whined.

'Yes,' said Jonathan, leaning on his walking stick. 'All the way back.'

'We can't give them back,' said Bouda. 'I stole the comb and the gold coin at the port of Camulodunum while we were hurrying through the crowds to the ship. I wouldn't even know the faces of the people I robbed.'

'Dear Lord.' Doctor Jonathan closed his eyes and pinched the top of his nose. 'Listen,' he said to Bouda. 'This must stop. No more stealing. Promise?'

Her head was still down but she nodded. 'I'll try.'

'Promise!'

'I promise.'

'Good.' The doctor nodded towards a stream on their right. 'Let's refill our waterskins and move on. I want to put as much distance between us and that man as possible.'

They walked in silence for three hours, paused for a brief lunch, then walked three more. Juba reckoned they had covered almost twenty miles that day.

The sun was throwing long shadows before them when they came to a humpbacked bridge over a small stream.

'Five miles to Colonia,' said Juba, reading a milestone shaped like an obelisk. 'Shall we press on?'

Ursula groaned and Gartha whined softly.

'I see an inn,' said Doctor Jonathan. 'Over by those woods. Shall we stay there? The girls in one room, Juba and I in another?'

Half an hour later they were eating a dinner of glutinous barley stew. Juba could feel Bouda's eyes on him but he was still angry and couldn't bear to look at her. Ursula was miserable because the innkeeper had made her put Gartha in the stables and charged them an extra quadrans. So they ate in silence and went glumly to their bedrooms.

Juba was lying on his bed staring at the ceiling when the doctor spoke.

'Don't judge her too harshly,' said Doctor Jonathan, and then added, almost under his breath, 'or me.'

'I thought she'd changed,' muttered Juba. 'Were all our discussions of philosophy and living a good life for nothing? I keep thinking of what Seneca says to Lucilius in his seventh letter: *A close friend obsessed with luxury only weakens us.*'

'There's a difference between studying a way of life and living it,' said the doctor. 'Don't forget: your lives are built on different foundations.'

'What do you mean?'

'You grew up in a place of safety, with wealth and two loving parents. For the first twelve years of your life nothing truly bad ever happened, correct?'

'I suppose.'

'So even when you were forced to leave your home in the middle of the night and flee with your brother and sisters to a

115

faraway province, you still had the sense that things might turn out all right. That is what I mean by a foundation.'

'And Bouda?'

'You tell me.'

'She grew up poor among a gang of cutpurses. She never knew her father, much less her mother.'

'Exactly,' said the doctor. 'Bouda had no foundation of safety. No assurance that her life would turn out well. Not even an assurance that she would survive. The only thing that makes her feel safe is mammon.'

'What's mammon?'

'It means material wealth.'

'*Gold and gems and pearls,*' Juba murmured, '*are the only things that keep you safe in this world.*'

'Is that what she says?'

'Yes. It's what her gang boss drilled into her.'

'Then can you blame her for stealing when she feels insecure?'

'No,' said Juba. 'I suppose not. It's just that I'd hoped she'd changed.'

He slept fitfully and when he dreamt it was of a little girl with red hair running from men who wanted to hurt her.

It seemed he had only just fallen asleep when Ursula was shaking him awake. 'Juba!' she said. 'Get up.'

'What?' He sat up and squinted at the small window of thick glass; it showed as a square of grey. 'It's still early. Let me sleep a little more.'

'Bouda's gone!' said Ursula. 'I got up to check on Gartha and her bed was empty.'

'Who's gone?' asked Doctor Jonathan, yawning.

'Bouda,' said Ursula.

'Probably just using the latrine.' Juba lay down again.

'No. Look what she left on her pillow.'

Juba opened his eyes and dimly saw the Minerva gem dangling a few inches from his face. He sat up again and took it. 'This was on her pillow?'

Ursula nodded.

He felt it like a blow to his heart. 'Then you're right: she is gone.'

For the first time in his life he really looked at the sardonyx cameo, bringing it close to the flickering flame of the oil-lamp on his bedside stool. He saw that Minerva's hair flowed out from beneath her helmet, wavy and reddish in the small flame. Her pale profile was lovely too. 'I never noticed before,' he murmured. 'But this Minerva looks just like Bouda.'

'We have to find her,' said Ursula.

'Yes,' said Juba. 'We're her foundation. We are all she has.'

'Finding her won't be easy,' said Doctor Jonathan from the window. 'The fog is as thick as last night's stew.'

They were silent for a moment. Then Juba looked at Ursula.

'Gartha can sniff her out!' he cried. 'Did she leave anything behind? Anything she's been wearing? Something Gartha can get her scent from?'

'Only the gem,' said Ursula. 'But the thong is leather. It might hold her scent.'

'I'll go now.' Juba started to do up his sandals.

'I'll come with you,' said Ursula.

'No,' said Juba. 'I'll be able to move faster on my own.' Then he added, 'I think I'm the reason she ran away and I'm the one who must convince her to come back.'

A short time later he was in the forecourt of the inn, holding the thong of the Minerva gem for Gartha to sniff. He had untied

117

the big dog's rope but kept hold of its end. 'Can you find Bouda?' he asked Gartha. 'Can you sniff her out?'

Gartha sniffed the Minerva gem on its leather thong, then put her nose down and swung it right and left. She pulled Juba across the courtyard and made the mist swirl as she searched for Bouda's scent. At the back door of the inn she found it, and Juba felt her tug on the rope. He let her lead him as she loped across the road and into the thick and foggy woods.

Chapter Twenty-One
CALIGO

It had been the hardest decision Bouda ever made in her life: to leave Juba and the Minerva gem behind.

The words of the philosopher Seneca floated into her head: *Even one instance of luxury or greed can do much harm.*

She gave a sobbing laugh. How true! Had she learned nothing over the winter months?

It seemed not.

Weeping, she ran blindly through the woods, letting the branches whip her legs and scratch her cheeks.

The almost-full moon went behind a cloud and suddenly the world was dark.

Above, below, before, behind.

She was a soul alone in a black abyss.

The terror of that emptiness brought her skidding to a halt. Her knees gave way and she clung to the trunk of a tree. The bark against her cheek was cool and smooth, so she slumped down to its base, keeping her arms around it. For once she understood Ursula's affection for trees. She knew without seeing that it was a silver birch, a tree whose nature spoke of mercy and grace.

She must have slept, for a rustling of ferns made her open her eyes to a foggy white morning.

A fox stood not two paces from her. A female, surely, looking back at her with golden eyes. The vixen's fur was coppery orange, rather than russet. The exact same colour of Bouda's hair before she had dyed it that ugly brown.

Another Latin proverb came into her head: *The fox can change her fur but not her nature.*

Bouda gave a bitter laugh. Startled, the vixen vanished into the ferns.

Bouda wept some more, but then a pang of hunger brought a stab of anxiety. How would she survive now? She had nothing. Nothing but the clothes on her back, the shoes on her feet and the folding knife around her wrist.

Why hadn't she kept the Minerva gem?

Because Flavia Gemina's last words had been echoing in her mind: *Juba loves what is good and noble. If you want to earn his love, you must seek the highest good . . .*

She wanted to show him that she wasn't all bad, that she could be virtuous.

Now she would have to go back to stealing after all.

Did she have any other options?

Yes, but they were worse. She did not want to beg and she would never sell her body. That was one reason she had run away from Tyranus.

Perhaps she could find work weaving or sewing. But it would not be the same if someone forced her to do it all day long. Then her freedom would be gone.

The sound of a wild animal moving through the bracken sent her heart leaping to her throat.

It sounded like something much bigger than a fox. Were there wolves here in Germania? Or bears?

Gripping the damp trunk of the slender birch, she pulled

herself up and backed out of the clearing into the bushes.

Then she turned and stumbled through damp knee-high brambles and around the trees. She tried to stay silent but she could hear her breath coming in gasps and her heart pounding.

The thing was still coming.

With a whimper of fear she pushed on, running blindly now in the foggy forest, trying to find her way back to the tavern and Juba.

Suddenly she tripped on a fallen branch and pitched forward into the damp ferns. When she recovered her breath she scrambled behind the trunk of an ancient beech. Pressing her back against it, she hugged her knees tightly, lowered her head and closed her eyes.

She prayed the creature would not find her.

It did. She smelled its meaty breath on her face and whimpered in fear.

But then, instead of teeth, she felt a hot tongue lathering her cheek. Bouda opened her eyes and almost sobbed with relief.

'Gartha!' She threw her arms around the warm, furry neck. 'How did you find me?'

'She's a scent-hound,' said Juba, emerging from between two trees. 'It's what she does.' He stood in his tawny-yellow birrus Britannicus, knee-deep in bracken with the fog swirling behind him, his black curls heavy with moisture. He looked tired but his sage-green eyes were full of compassion.

Bouda buried her face in Gartha's fur. 'Go away,' she said.

'I can't,' he said softly. 'You and I have unfinished business.'

'I gave back the gem!' she cried, her voice muffled by Gartha's fur.

She heard the rustle of ferns as he sat on the ground beside her.

'Do you remember a few months ago when Doctor Jonathan was teaching us the philosophy of Jesus? How sometimes you have to give up something in order to gain it?'

Bouda did not reply but a spark of hope flared in her heart and she opened her eyes.

She felt his warm breath in her ear as he leaned even closer. 'I've come to give it back to you,' he said. 'It's yours.'

She stayed still, hardly daring to breathe.

'What do you mean?' she said.

'I was going to give it to you back at Caudex's villa in Verulamium,' he said. 'It was to be a betrothal gift. But now it's yours whether you agree to marry me or not.'

She lifted her face from Gartha's warm neck and looked at him in wonder. 'You want to marry me?'

He nodded. 'I have for a long time,' he said. 'Almost from the first moment I saw you.'

'Why?'

'Your courage, your spirit and your beauty.'

She gave a sobbing laugh and once more hid her face in patient Gartha's neck. 'I'm not very beautiful at the moment.' Her voice was muffled by dog fur. 'My horrible brown hair and swollen eyes.'

'Bouda,' he said. 'You will always be beautiful to me. Because I see your soul. If you marry me, I will never willingly leave you again. If you want to go your own way, you can.' He pressed the Minerva gem into her hand. 'But this is yours. No matter what you decide.'

She let go of Gartha and took the gem and held it in her cupped hands. For a moment they both looked at it in silence.

'She's beautiful,' said Bouda. 'She looks so kind and wise.'

'She looks like you.'

'Minerva? Or the little Medusa on her aegis?' She gave him a mischievous glance.

He laughed. 'The goddess, of course, with her lovely profile and wavy red hair.'

Then he grew serious and took her hands in his, closing them over the gem.

'So, will you?' he asked. 'Will you marry me? The gem is yours to keep whatever you say.'

She left her hands in his for a moment, then pulled them free and handed him the priceless gem on its sturdy leather thong. Turning her back to him, she lifted up her hair.

'Put it on me?'

She waited for a long moment. Then he put the necklace on her and she could feel the tips of his fingers warm against the back of her neck as he fastened the clasp.

'There,' he said. And his fingers moved away.

She let her hair down but did not turn around.

'The coin I dedicated a year ago at the spring of Sulis Minerva,' she said, 'was for you. The nettle-cloth I sewed for Fronto was his consolation because I loved you, not him. The reason I cared for Ursula when she had a fever was because she is your sister and I care for you. When I'm with you,' she said, 'you make me want to be a better person. So yes, Lucius Domitius Juba. I will marry you.'

Then she turned and took his face in her hands and kissed him.

Chapter Twenty-Two
COLONIA

A warm summer sun had burnt the fog away when Ursula saw Gartha lope out of the dark German woods. A moment later, Juba and Bouda emerged after her.

'Look!' she cried to Doctor Jonathan. 'They're holding hands!'

The doctor looked up from his scroll. He and Ursula were sitting at a beechwood table in the sunny forecourt of the Inn of the Limping Goat. Ursula got up and ran to meet Gartha, who put her paws on Ursula's shoulders and covered her face with kisses. 'Good dog!' cried Ursula. 'Did you play Cupid?'

Gartha panted happily and it seemed to Ursula that she was grinning.

Juba and Bouda came up a few moments later, still holding hands and smiling shyly.

'Sit and have breakfast,' said Jonathan. 'I've just ordered us some hot porridge and weak beer. And sausage for those of us who aren't vegetarians. If we set off soon, we should make Colonia by midday.'

'We're betrothed,' said Juba, his voice husky.

'The Minerva gem is to be my dowry,' added Bouda.

'*Euge!*' squealed Ursula, jumping up and down. She hugged Juba and then Bouda.

A plump blonde serving girl came up with a bowl of steaming barley porridge and two ceramic beakers on a tray.

'If you're betrothed,' said the doctor, 'then I think we can stretch to celebratory raisins on our porridge. Bring some raisins for the porridge?' he said to the girl. 'Also two more weak beers?'

They were finishing the porridge when Gartha stood up and wagged her tail. She was looking towards the humpbacked bridge to the west, the way they had come the day before. A mule-drawn carruca had just come over it and was rattling towards them. It was brightly coloured with a yellow body, red wheels and a sky-blue canvas top stretched over hoops. Ursula had never seen it before, but the driver looked familiar: a slender, dark-haired woman in an orange tunic.

Beside the female driver sat a small white dog wearing a conical felt cap of saffron yellow.

'Issa!' cried Ursula, waving both arms above her head. 'And Clio! Lupus Pantomimus and his troupe are here in Belgica!'

'Germania Inferior,' said Juba, wiping his mouth with his napkin. 'We've been in this province for over two weeks.'

But Ursula ignored him. Little Issa was already off the wagon and scampering towards them, her belled collar jingling. She and Gartha sniffed each other and wagged their tails. Ursula and the others laughed at the sight of the huge scent-hound and the little lapdog.

Now Ursula saw three figures coming over the humpbacked bridge on foot: a skinny dark-haired man in a sea-green tunic, a youth in a nut-brown cloak that matched his hair and a silver-blonde girl in lavender.

'Lupus!' cried Doctor Jonathan.

When the skinny man in sea-green heard them calling and saw them waving from their table, he ran towards them, finishing with a triple somersault and landing in a spray of gravel. Lupus and Jonathan kissed and then embraced, slapping each other hard on the backs. Bircha, the silver-blonde flute player, and her brother, Bolianus the drummer, came hurrying up a few moments later.

When Clio climbed down from the driver's seat, Ursula squealed again. 'Clio! You're pregnant! When's it due?'

Lupus proudly put his arm around his wife and held up four fingers, which Ursula guessed stood for months.

'We've just put on a private show for a rich Roman lady near here,' said Bircha breathlessly. 'We're on our way back to Colonia. Fronto will be so glad to see you. You must stay with us.'

'As soon as we get home I'll tell Fronto and Vindex you're here!' Bolianus ran his hand through his feathery brown hair.

An hour later Clio reined in the mules and the others stopped walking as she pointed to a city on the horizon.

'There it is,' said Bolianus. 'Colonia Claudia Ara Agrippinensium.'

'Look how high the city walls are!' said Ursula.

'Nearly thirty feet high,' said Bolianus. 'With nine gates and twenty-one towers. You can't see it from here,' he added, 'but the river Rhinus is on the far side.'

'That river forms one of the borders of the Roman Empire,' murmured Juba.

'We're renting a house just inside the Western Gate,' said Clio. She flicked the mules into motion. Tombs began to appear on the side of the road, becoming bigger and more majestic as they approached the now-looming wall. The road was crowded with carts and wagons, but traffic moved briskly as a pair of soldiers waved them through the red sandstone arch of the gate.

Presently Clio turned off the main road and stopped the wagon in front of a row of whitewashed huts. Lupus helped her down, then silently pointed at some stables a little further up the road. He led the mules and wagon that way while the rest of them went inside one of the houses.

Made of wattle and daub with a thatched roof, a beaten earth floor and a central fire, it was like a British roundhouse in every respect but one: it was square. The most expensive item in the house was a bronze cauldron hanging from an iron firedog. A little girl of about seven ran to hug Bircha and Clio, but hid behind Bircha's tunic when she saw Gartha, even though Ursula had taken off the scent-hound's mane, lest the sentries be alarmed.

'This is Hestia,' said Bircha, stroking the little girl's fair hair. 'We found her begging by the side of the road when we first arrived and Clio insisted we adopt her.'

'Don't be afraid of Gartha,' said Ursula. 'She loves children.'

Little Hestia cautiously approached Gartha, who was now resting in her sphinx pose, and as Hestia stroked the big dog's panting head, Bolianus gestured around.

'We're only living here,' he explained, 'until we can find a bigger house. In the meantime, this one is handy; there's a stable nearby for the pantomine wagon and mules.'

Bircha pointed at some low beds against the back wall in the darkest part of the one-roomed house. 'We sleep there.'

Ursula saw a partly unrolled rush mat hanging from the ceiling; it could screen off the beds if needed. In one of the front corners of the house was a table for food preparation near some shelves of jars, bags and bottles. In the other front corner was a chamber pot and bucket of water. Again, a hanging mat screened this off from the rest of the house. With only two small windows and a doorway, the house was dim, but it was warm, dry and cosy.

'I'm going to go to the barracks and tell Fronto and Vindex that we're back,' said Bolianus, taking his cloak from a peg near the door. 'And that his sister and brother have just arrived along with his future sister-in-law.'

He went out through the wooden door, leaving it open to let in more light.

Ursula was helping Bircha prepare lunch by slicing sausage, with Gartha sitting attentively nearby, when the light in the house dimmed.

Two soldiers stood in the open doorway.

'Fronto? Vindex?' Ursula squinted as she ran to them. But they were not archers of the Hamian cohort; they were Roman legionaries with unsmiling faces and a businesslike manner.

'Lucius Domitius Juba?' said one, consulting a wax tablet. 'Domitia Ursula? Bouda, great-granddaughter of Boudica? I have a warrant for your arrest.' Ursula felt an almost physical blow to her heart. Just when she believed all her prayers had been answered, Domitian's agents had finally caught up with them.

Chapter Twenty-Three
TRAIANUS

The first time Bouda saw the man who would one day be known as Rome's best and greatest ruler, she was not impressed.

As the two soldiers led them into an opulent room of the vast Praetorium, a man wearing the white cloak of a commander rose from behind a marble desk. 'My name is Marcus Ulpius Traianus,' he said, 'but you can call me Trajan.'

Bouda had been raised by a powerful and charismatic gangboss called Tyranus, the Tyrant.

She had met Juba's uncle, Pantera, another dangerous, rich and attractive man who smelled of power.

Even fat Montanus, sponsor of the games they had taken part in the previous year, was more interesting than this tall man with thin lips and grey hair combed over his forehead.

Although the commander looked Roman, he spoke Latin with an accent. He reminded Bouda of a Spanish clerk from an auction house in Londinium. He acted like one, too, for he walked around each of them slowly, looking them up and down and making notes on a wax tablet.

'Not bad,' he said as he circled Bouda. 'Lovely face and skin, stunning eyes. But the hair is too drab. Not good enough for the Emperor.'

As he turned away, Bouda remembered that Trajan was the name of the commander who had rushed from Spain to help the Emperor squash a rebellion against him.

'Intriguing,' said Trajan as he examined Ursula. 'A girl disguised as a boy. Nice combination of skin, eyes and hair, but I can tell by that spark in her eyes that she would be trouble.'

He spent the most time examining Juba.

'Very attractive,' he said. 'The same sage-green eyes and nutmeg-coloured skin as your sister. Most appealing in an adolescent.' Bouda saw Juba flinch as the commander stroked his cheek. 'Good. No beard yet. How old are you? Fifteen?'

'Not until the middle of December.'

'Perfect.'

'Perfect for what?' asked Juba in a shaky voice. But Trajan had strolled back to his desk.

'Lucius Domitius Juba.' Still standing, the legate touched a sheet of papyrus with the tips of his long fingers. 'The Emperor Domitian issued a warrant for the arrest of you and your siblings more than a year and a half ago. It amazes me that you have eluded his agents for so long.' He found another piece of papyrus and frowned down at it, then looked up. 'I presume the girl with the dyed brown hair standing beside you is the one who styles herself as Boudica's great-granddaughter?'

For the first time his gaze locked with Bouda's.

Bouda caught her breath. It was like stepping into the tepidarium and finding it piping hot instead of lukewarm. Trajan's jet-black eyes were full of keen intelligence.

'My report says this girl has sworn to avenge Boudica's death.'

Bouda felt Juba stiffen beside her. From the corner of her eye she saw him lower his eyes.

Before Juba could reply, Trajan lifted his forefinger.

'Don't lie to me, young man,' he said. 'That is the one thing I will not forgive. And before you speak, know this: there are many of us who hate the Emperor and cannot wait to see a better man in his place.'

Juba looked up sharply.

'So tell me the truth,' said the commander, 'and I will judge if you are my enemy or my ally.' He nodded at Bouda. 'Begin by telling me who she is.'

No! Don't tell him! Bouda was screaming at him in her thoughts. *It's a trap!*

But Juba did not hear her thoughts.

'You are correct, sir,' he replied. 'Bouda is a British girl of the Iceni tribe who claims to be the descendant of Queen Boudica. But she has never harmed any Roman. In fact, she has risked her life to avert bloodshed.'

Bouda could not remain silent any longer. 'I'm not even certain if Boudica really is my great-grandmother,' she said. 'It's just what—'

'*Tac!*' The commander held up a thin forefinger. 'Do not address me until I address you.' He turned his keen gaze back to Juba. 'Tell me, young man – and remember that your future depends upon it – are you for or against Domitian, our glorious lord and god?'

Don't trust him! Bouda was thinking. *It's a trick to get you to betray Domitian.*

Beside her, Juba was quiet for a long moment. Then he spoke.

'My parents died two summers ago, sir. A man in our household, someone we trusted, denounced them. He falsely

131

accused them of being disloyal. One night, Domitian sent his Praetorian Guard to arrest us and to confiscate all our wealth. My parents distracted the soldiers long enough to give us time to escape. Then they drank hemlock rather than betray us under torture. I saw their bodies as I was fleeing.'

Juba lifted his chin. 'They were still young and had many years of life ahead of them. Domitian stole those years from them. I will never forget that.' Juba took a deep breath and closed his eyes for a moment. When he had regained his composure he looked directly at Trajan. 'With every fibre of my being I am against Domitian. I hate him to the tips of my fingers.'

Bouda gasped but Trajan ignored her.

'Tell me,' he said to Juba. 'If certain men banded together to depose the tyrant and find a better man to take his place, would you be for them or against?'

'It's not that simple,' said Juba. 'In theory I would help them, but in practice I must put the safety of my sisters first.'

'Sisters?' Trajan looked down at the document on his desk.

'I have another sister,' said Juba. 'She was five months old the night we fled.' He hung his head. 'We were robbed on our way to Ostia so I traded her for passage to Britannia. I left her with a woman who had just lost her own baby. That woman promised to raise her well. I don't want to do anything that might endanger my little sister or the people who took her in.'

Trajan's face was unreadable. He turned to Ursula. 'And you?' he said. 'What do you think of our Emperor?'

'I love Domitian!' said Ursula.

'Beg pardon?'

'I love our lord and god, Domitian,' Ursula replied firmly.

Trajan raised an eyebrow. 'You love the man who caused your parents' death and sent you into exile?'

'Yes,' said Ursula. 'Because my God teaches us to love our enemies. I pray for him every day,' she added.

Bouda thought she saw a flicker of amusement in his eyes.

'Are you a follower of the Way?' Trajan asked Ursula. 'Like the doctor with whom you are travelling?'

For once, Ursula was speechless.

'No matter.' Trajan turned to Bouda. 'And you?' he said.

Bouda hesitated. Should she tell the truth? Or lie? She chose the second option. 'I have no opinion. I am just a girl.'

The commander gave a snort of disgust. 'Take the girls away,' he said to the two soldiers. 'Send them back to their friends. But the boy stays.'

No! Don't hurt Juba! cried Bouda in her thoughts. But she was too afraid to say anything out loud.

As one of the guards put his hand on her arm to guide her from the room, she shot Juba a pleading look of apology for not standing by him. But he kept his face expressionless and his eyes straight ahead.

When Bouda and Ursula emerged into the bright space of the courtyard she gasped with relief, like a swimmer coming up for air. The soldiers stopped after a few paces.

'You are free to go,' said one of them, and he gestured for them to continue out of the governor's palace.

Ursula ran across the vast courtyard of the Praetorium towards the monumental exit, which led back into the town. So she did not see what they were surely meant to see: a sight that made Bouda's blood run cold.

A tall man in a hooded black cloak had emerged from a room on the right and was walking across the courtyard. As he passed by, he turned his head slightly to look at her.

It was the closest Bouda had ever come to fainting.

133

The hooded man wore a gilded mask with terrible black eyeholes.

It was Tortor, the Emperor Domitian's most sadistic torturer.

He had caught up with them at last and he was heading for the room where Juba was being held prisoner.

Chapter Twenty-Four
FASCIAE

When Ursula ran through the open door into the one-room house she skidded to a halt at the sight of Bircha the ex-Druid girl in the arms of a soldier. But when her eyes adjusted to the dimness she saw it was her brother without his fish-scale armour.

'Fronto!' she cried.

Bircha pulled back, blushing, even though they were married. Fronto turned with a smile but it faded when he saw Ursula's face.

'What's the matter?' he said. 'Where's Juba?'

'Oh, Fronto!' cried Ursula. 'Some soldiers took us to an important man and he questioned us. Then he let me and Bouda go but he kept Juba because he confessed he was an enemy of you-know-who!'

Gartha came up, tail wagging, and Ursula bent to hug her woolly neck.

'What important man?' Fronto let go of Bircha and took a step towards Ursula.

'I don't remember his name.' Ursula stood up, but kept a hand on Gartha's head. 'I think it started with a T.'

'Trajan,' said Bouda, stepping into the hut. Her face was

deathly pale. 'It was the commander named Trajan. But that's not the worst of it. Tortor is in there with them.'

Ursula turned with a gasp. 'Tortor from Camulodunum?'

'Tortor?' said Fronto with a puzzled look.

Bouda nodded. 'Three days after your wedding, Flavia Gemina came to tell us to flee Britannia because Domitian had sent his official torturer to arrest us.' Bouda wrung her hands. 'And now he's caught us and he's going to hurt Juba!'

'Where's Doctor Jonathan?' asked Ursula, looking around. 'And Lupus and Clio and Bolianus?'

'They went to the stables to pray,' said Bircha. 'The walls are thin here and their religion is frowned upon. Fronto only returned a few moments before you got here,' she added. 'I didn't even have time to tell him what happened.'

Fronto went to the bed and picked up his heavy fish-scale armour. He slipped it over his head and then put on his belt and his white-plumed conical helmet. 'I'll go ask for an audience with Trajan now,' he said. 'Maybe I can help.'

'Or maybe they'll torture you, too!' cried Bircha, clinging to his arm. 'You've kept your identity a secret until now. Don't risk everything.'

'I have to,' said Fronto with a wobbly smile.

Ursula stared at her brother in amazement. Two years ago he had been a strange boy obsessed with signs and omens. But the army had turned him into a brave soldier. She felt an unbearable mixture of pride and anguish.

'I'll go to the governor's palace with you,' said Ursula.

'Me, too,' said Bouda, nearly in tears.

'I'll wait here with Hestia and Gartha,' said Bircha. 'I'll pray to my gods too.'

*

136

It was a market day, and the Via Praetoria was crowded with stallholders now packing up the remains of their wares and dismantling their stalls. By the time they reached the Praetorium at the other end of the city, nearly an hour had passed since Ursula had last seen Juba. She tried not to think what torment he might have been suffering during that time.

Fronto was heading towards one of the soldiers on guard outside the palace when Bouda screamed.

Following her gaze, Ursula screamed too.

Juba stood in the monumental entrance, alone and unguarded.

His head was bound with of strips of linen, so that it seemed he was wearing a white helmet. Ursula almost fainted when she saw that the bandages on top were stained with blood.

Chapter Twenty-Five
INSIDIAE

Bouda screamed again at the sight of the bloody bandages on Juba's head.

'Shhh! It's all right.' He gave them all a weak smile. 'It's not as bad as it looks. They said it will heal in a few days.'

'Oh, Juba!' Bouda threw her arms around him. 'Thank Minerva you're all right! I'm so sorry. I'm a coward!'

'You're not a coward,' he said gently. 'You said what you had to. Domitian is not your enemy; he's ours.' He held her for a few moments and then released her.

'Fronto.' He gripped his brother's shoulders. 'Are you well?'

Fronto nodded. 'But what did they do to you?'

Juba shook his head and glanced around the crowded street. 'Where can we talk?'

'The others are in the stables, praying,' whispered Ursula. 'Back that way.'

Bouda held Juba's hand all the way down the busy Via Praetoria and only let go when they stopped at the house to collect Bircha and Gartha. The stables had brick walls, a tile roof and a bright inner courtyard. Inside, a kind-looking blond man with a beard gestured towards a corner storeroom.

The sweet scent of barley, sour mash and straw filled Bouda's head as she entered the dim space. The storeroom obviously doubled as a meeting room, for there were her friends, sitting on bales of hay arranged in a circle.

Doctor Jonathan was the first to catch sight of them. 'Juba!' He used his walking stick to push himself up from a bale of hay. 'What have they done to you?'

'Oh, Juba!' cried Clio. She was holding Issa and came forward with Lupus, who was giving Juba his bug-eyed look of enquiry. Bolianus stood, too, his mouth hanging open.

'Don't worry,' said Juba. 'They didn't hurt me.'

'Of course they hurt you.' Doctor Jonathan examined the top of Juba's bandaged head. 'It's stained with blood!'

'It's really all right.' Juba lowered his voice. 'It turns out they are on our side. Even Tortor.'

Bircha closed the storeroom door behind her, plunging them all into deep gloom, for the only windows were high and small.

As Bouda's eyes adjusted to the darkness, she saw Jonathan's eyebrows go up. 'The torturer is working against . . . Remus?' Even though they were now in a dim, soundproof room, he used their code name for Domitian.

'Yes,' said Juba.

'What about Prasutus?' asked Ursula. 'Tortor was about to prod him with a red-hot poker in the port of Camulodunum!'

'Tortor says he wasn't actually going to burn him,' replied Juba, 'only singe the wool. He had to convince Montanus that he was still loyal to Domitian, you see. And I believe him.'

'If he didn't torture you then why is there blood on your dressing?' asked Doctor Jonathan.

Juba sighed and sat on one of the bales of hay.

'Yes,' said Bouda, sitting beside him. 'What did they do to you?'

'They shaved my head and gave me a mark,' he said. 'A kind of tattoo.'

'A tattoo?' Bouda's stomach flipped at the thought of them cutting into Juba's scalp.

'Like a slave?' cried Ursula.

'Yes. Except when my hair grows back you won't be able to see it. Until then I'm to tell people I hurt my head and keep it bandaged.'

'The Ancient Greeks used that method to smuggle information behind enemy lines,' said Fronto.

Lupus grunted, *Why?*

'Why did they give me the mark? Because I've agreed to help overthrow Remus.'

'Who are "they"?' Fronto asked. 'Who are you helping?'

Juba lowered his voice even more. 'An important commander named Trajan. He and some others have found men willing to assassinate Dom— Remus. And they even have a man in Rome who's agreed to be Emperor. He's a good man, according to Trajan, and he'll make a good ruler. I'm going to help them,' he added. 'You can stay here in Colonia with Bircha and Bolianus.' In the dim storeroom, the whites of his eyes gleamed first on Bouda and then on Ursula. 'But tomorrow I'm setting out for Rome.'

They all stared at him.

'But you could die,' Bouda whispered, clutching his hand.

'It's possible.' He gave her hand a reassuring squeeze. 'But I can't marry you if I can't respect myself,' he said. 'I'm tired of running. It's time to take action.'

In the darkness, Bouda saw Doctor Jonathan shake his head. 'It is never right to kill another man in cold blood.'

'I'm not going to kill him,' said Juba. 'If all goes according to plan my only job is to make sure he has no weapons at hand.'

Bouda frowned. 'What did they do to you to change your heart?'

'It wasn't what they did to me. It was what they said to me.'

'What did they say?' asked Fronto.

Juba took a deep breath. 'They told me that Domitian has Dora.'

'Dora?' cried Fronto.

Ursula gasped. 'Our Dora?'

'Your little sister?' asked Bouda.

Juba nodded. 'Trajan told me that the Emperor collects interesting-looking children to be his companions. He used to have a boy with a freakishly small head. He took that boy to the games and even asked his advice in matters of state. When the boy died last year the Emperor started looking for replacements. Since then he has kidnapped or bought half a dozen children.'

Juba paused and Bouda heard him take a breath. 'But this is the terrible thing: Trajan told me that Domitian's youngest slave is a two-year-old girl with brown skin and tight black curls. He calls her Dora.'

'Dora!' gasped Bouda.

'No!' wailed Ursula. 'It can't be!'

Fronto made the sign against evil.

'That's not all.' Juba's voice was husky. 'Apparently, Dora's duties include emptying the Emperor's chamber pot and washing his feet.'

Everyone groaned. Then Ursula said through clenched teeth, 'If you're going to Rome to rescue baby Dora, then I'm coming, too!'

Bouda's heart was thudding. 'Me, too,' she said.

'Really?' Juba stared at her.

141

'Yes,' said Bouda. 'After I saw Tortor, I made a vow to Minerva that if you came back unharmed I would never abandon you again.'

Lupus grunted and Clio said, 'We're coming too. What about you, Bolianus? Bircha?'

Bircha gave a tiny shake of her head and took Fronto's hand.

'Bircha and I are just getting settled,' said Fronto. 'I'd love her to stay with me. But I can try to find out if Trajan really is against Domitian. If I hear otherwise, I promise we will send you a warning.'

'I'll stay, too,' said Bolianus. 'And bring you any news, if needed.'

'How will you live?' Clio asked Bircha and Bolianus. 'And what will we do without our flute player and drummer?'

'I already give Bircha most of my pay each month,' said Fronto.

Bolianus said to Clio, 'Surely you can find other musicians here?'

Bouda had a sudden idea. 'Why don't I learn to play the flute?'

Ursula nodded. 'And I can bang a tambourine or drum.'

Bouda looked at Bircha and Bolianus. 'Will you loan us your instruments?'

'Of course,' they replied, and Bircha added, 'Keep them!'

'Then it's decided,' said Juba, rising to his feet. 'We're all going to Rome. Everyone except Fronto, Bircha and Bolianus.'

'Doctor Jonathan?' said Ursula. 'Are you still coming with us?'

They all looked at the doctor. He was still sitting on his bale of hay, head down, and gripping his walking stick.

Finally he raised his head and looked at Juba. 'Very well. But

I say again; I will not take part in any murder, assassination or killing of any kind. And I will not give you the information you so desperately want to know.'

Juba gave a bitter bark of laughter.

'What?' Bouda gave him a questioning look.

'Trajan already knows the date,' said Juba. 'His spies in Rome told him. That's what he's tattooed on my head: the date of the tyrant's death. It's both a sign to the conspirators that I am with them, and an insurance against my betraying them.'

Chapter Twenty-Six
ODYSSEY

I t was fitting, thought Juba, that Lupus's troupe was performing a version of Homer's *Odyssey* most evenings, for like Odysseus they were making their way home. And like Odysseus when he arrived at Ithaca, they were in disguise.

There was no point hurrying, Trajan had told him, for the day of the assassination was more than three months away. '*Be like the tortoise in Aesop's fable*,' the commander had advised Juba at their memorable meeting in Colonia. '*If you go slow and steady you will win the race.*'

Their only task now was to avoid capture or death and reach Rome by the appointed day.

For the first time, Juba felt he was not running from something but moving towards a goal.

The only thing that caused him anguish was the thought of his little sister Dora having to empty the imperial chamber pot and rub lotion on Domitian's feet.

And so, to the sound of throbbing cicadas, they moved steadily south, through vineyards, villages and fragrant fields of lavender. The days grew longer and the nights were warm.

Bouda no longer pretended to be the doctor's wife. She learned to play the flute and was a brown-haired pantomime musician.

Ursula also became a musician. She shook the tambourine or banged the drum during Lupus's shows, and the rest of the time she assisted Doctor Jonathan.

Juba's dramatic bandages attracted people's attention so he abandoned the role of a slave. Now he played the part of a grateful patient devoted to the man who had saved his life.

After every pantomime show, people showed their appreciation. Sometimes they gave a coin or two, but mostly they brought food: a loaf of bread, a basket of fruit, a slab of goat's cheese, a grape-leaf packet of black olives, a small jar of olive oil or honey. They even brought meat: a chicken from the farmyard or a piece of roast lamb left over from a sacrifice.

Gartha received marrowbones and hard tack.

Once a woman left a little pouch with a bone needle and thread. A man left a bath set: a strigil on a ring, along with tweezers, an ear-scoop and a fingernail cleaner.

After every performance, while it was still light, Doctor Jonathan sat to take people's pulses and offer a brief word of advice about diet, sleep or purging. For the first time Juba realised that the doctor only charged what people could afford. If a man was rich, Jonathan would ask a fair price: a leg of lamb, a wheel of cheese, a new cloak or even coins. But if the patient was poor he would take only a token payment, such as a heel of bread, a tiny coin, and once even a pine cone.

In late July they heard about games to be held at the new amphitheatre of Nemausus and decided to take a detour to watch them. Juba was not due to meet his contact until mid-September and travellers coming from the capital assured them that Rome was no more than four weeks by foot.

In the ancient town of Nemausus, in an amphitheatre almost as big as Rome's, they watched a beast hunt and gladiator combats and acrobats on chariots. There was even a re-enactment of the Battle of Actium with ships on wheels and a beautiful slave-girl playing the part of Cleopatra.

As Juba watched the boat move across the sand, dramatically rushing the Egyptian queen to her dying lover, he felt Bouda take his hand.

'Tyranus lied to me!' she whispered.

He looked at her questioningly.

'He told me that gold and gems and pearls keep you safe.' She pointed at the man playing the part of Anthony down in the arena. The actor was pretending to stab himself in the stomach, to show how the famous general had taken his own life. 'Wealth couldn't keep Marcus Antonius safe,' she said. 'Or Cleopatra.'

Juba shook his head in mock despair. 'That's what I was teaching in our classes on the Stoics all winter,' he said. 'And what I told you about my parents in the hay-cart our last night in Britannia.'

'I know. But it's different when you see it. Oh!'

Her gasp was echoed by thousands of others as the slave-girl playing Cleopatra brought a fake asp out of a basket and let it bite her throat. Then she 'died' dramatically on the sand.

Juba squeezed her hand. 'See?' he said. 'Honour meant more to Cleopatra than wealth or power, and even life itself.'

Chapter Twenty-Seven
AESTAS

Bouda never forgot that golden summer.

The cool blue mornings were as fresh as diving into water. Then the sun's chariot rose over the horizon and filled the world with heat. Trembling poplar trees lined ribbon-straight roads under the high blue sky. Sometimes they passed vineyards that stretched as far as the eye could see, or fragrant fields of lavender.

Most days they would stop to lunch in the shade of a tree. Their basic lunch was a shared loaf of bread and water from a brook. Sometimes they added olives and whenever they had cheese Ursula would quote Epicurus, her favourite philosopher next to Jesus. *'Cheese is enough to turn bread and water into a feast.'*

After a short siesta during the hottest part of the day, they would resume walking through the afternoon, golden and throbbing with the creak of cicadas.

One day early in the summer, Bouda's pale skin had become red and hot. Later, she had been sick in the bushes

'Your fair skin isn't use to this sun,' Doctor Jonathan had told her. 'Put on this ointment and tomorrow we'll have a rest day in the shade.'

Clio had taken her inside their wagon. 'Choose either that parasol or that straw sunhat. And just wear your long-sleeved undertunic.'

Bouda had chosen the straw sunhat and shed her tartan tunic in favour of just her white nettle-cloth undertunic. It was gauzy and light and let in the breeze but not the sun.

From then on she was also careful to walk or sit in shade wherever possible.

Although the pantomime wagon was with them, they mainly used it for storage. This was partly to save the mules' hooves but also because it didn't go much faster than a person on foot and was not comfortable to ride in. Clio was now heavily pregnant and sometimes sat at the front and held the reins. But the mules could follow them with no driver at all.

Under the golden sun and blue skies of Gallia Narbonensis, Bouda finally understood why long marches were Fronto's favourite part of being a soldier.

There was something about constantly moving forward that filled her with joy. She felt both free and in control. She loved the feel of the road beneath her feet and the sun on her hat and the gift of a soft breeze that fluttered her tunic and hair and made the tiny drops of perspiration cool her face.

Sometimes she walked hand in hand with Juba, whose bandages had finally come off to show his tightly curled black hair. Sometimes she walked alone at the front or the rear. Occasionally, big silent Gartha, their lion-dog protector, would pad beside her, panting pinkly. Doctor Jonathan and Lupus and now Juba were skilled with a sling. Every few days one of them would go into the woods with Gartha. Hunter and scent-hound would return a few hours later with a rabbit or some game birds, and once even a small deer. All of them except vegetarian Ursula feasted on roast venison that night.

They each wore out at least three pairs of shoes, but luckily cobblers got sick and needed treatment too. And they had enough coins to pay if the local cobbler was healthy. They stored their overtunics in the wagon and only used their woollen cloaks at night for blankets.

One day in August, Bouda saw the Mediterranean for the first time. Its peacock blue made her eyes open wide to receive its particles, and her soul drank in its infinite beauty.

Soon they were following the coast to avoid the high mountains. Sometimes after their midday meal they would walk across a sandy beach into the shallows – even pregnant Clio and big Gartha – and splash in water as transparent as glass. They kept on their undertunics, which dried almost at once. Afterwards, Bouda's skin was silky with sea-salt and once when Juba kissed her she could taste the salt on his lips.

'None of that!' chided Ursula, waggling her forefinger. 'You're not married yet.'

Then they were in Italy.

Bouda fingered the Minerva jewel that nestled in the hollow at the base of her throat. 'Dear Minerva,' she whispered, 'thank you for bringing me to Italy. Please keep protecting us and help us rescue baby Dora.'

Elegant parasol pine trees – resin-scented and full of creaking cicadas – provided perfume and music. The sea dazzled their eyes, in shades ranging from glass green to lapis lazuli to dark blue cobalt. The wine was so red it was almost black. The grapes on their vines were still tart and green, but the figs were already ripening into purple.

In many towns the local people had tawny hair and some even had blue eyes.

'I think that's the town our mother is from,' said Juba one day, looking across a valley to a hill town.

'Oh, let's go there!' cried Ursula.

'Better not,' said Juba. 'We don't want to get any of them in trouble by association.'

It was just as well they didn't divert, because Clio had a dizzy spell and Doctor Jonathan prescribed three days' rest. Afterwards they had to go more slowly and covered only five miles per day instead of the usual ten or twelve.

In Florentia, Jonathan performed a cataract operation by pushing a bronze needle into the white part of a man's eyeball. With Juba holding the man's head and Ursula assisting with wool, egg white and bandages, Jonathan drained the excess humours. 'I can see!' cried the man and kissed the doctor's feet.

A week later, in an ancient Etruscan spa town fifty miles from Rome, Clio went into labour and gave birth to a little boy. Mother and child were healthy but Jonathan prescribed rest for at least a week, so the four of them said farewell to Clio and Lupus and went on without the pantomime wagon.

Because of this delay they did not reach Ostia until two days after the Ides of September, three days before the predicted date of Domitian's doom. They arrived lean and brown from walking more than fifteen hundred miles, their heads full of the people they had met and the things they had seen.

As they came across the bridge from the necropolis of Isola Sacra, the first autumn rains pelted them with watery arrows.

The storm passed quickly and a rainbow came out along with the rich smell of damp earth.

But now there was a different feel in the air. A breath of

sadness as the first leaves skittered before them on the road and clouds loomed on the horizon.

On that day they finally discovered what had happened to baby Dora and those who had adopted her.

And Bouda knew that her golden summer was finally over.

III

Chapter Twenty-Eight
OSTIA

It was Ursula who recognised the old woman begging by a fountain near Ostia's Marina Gate.

They had spent the night in Portus and set out at dawn. Bouda would not go on the ferry so they had to go upstream to cross the bridge and only arrived in Ostia late in the morning, their clothes already dry after the rainstorm. They went straight to the apartment block where baby Dora's foster family lived. Located near the Marina Gate, it was a red-brick building four storeys tall, with balconies inside rather than outside so that residents could look into a big central courtyard. But none of the neighbours seemed to know Calpurnia Firma or her dark-skinned husband. And they had never heard of a brown-skinned baby girl.

'It was only two years ago!' cried Ursula, her eyes blazing. 'How could they not remember her?'

'It's almost as if someone has threatened them,' said Juba.

'Of course they've been threatened,' said Bouda, pulling her cloak around her shoulders. 'I recognise the look in their eyes: it's fear. We'll probably never find out what happened to the people who were raising your little sister.'

They were standing on the busy pavement outside the

Marina Apartments. Doctor Jonathan gripped his walking stick with both hands and gazed down at his feet. 'Maybe it's better if we don't find out,' he said.

Juba nodded and clenched his jaw. 'We know who has baby Dora now. That's all that matters.'

'Doctor Jonathan,' said Ursula. 'I'm hungry.'

'Me, too,' said Bouda. 'We haven't eaten since yesterday at noon.'

'I know.' Doctor Jonathan looked around. 'Master of the Universe, how little this place has changed! I wonder if the Peacock Tavern is still open. When I was a boy they served the best chickpea pancakes in Ostia and they had a little inner courtyard shaded by a grape arbour. It's not far. Near the north end of the forum, if I remember correctly.'

'Can we go there?' said Ursula. 'I'm famished.'

Jonathan led the way, his walking stick in his right hand and his medical satchel bouncing against his left hip.

Juba and Bouda followed behind him, holding hands, while Ursula and Gartha took up the rear. As they passed a fountain, Gartha stopped to drink. She put her big paws up on the marble rim and lapped noisily, slopping water on to the pavement.

Somewhere nearby an animal began whining pathetically. Ursula looked around for a wounded dog. But she only saw a barefoot old beggar-woman sitting on the ground. With a shiver of horror, she realised the dog-like whining was coming from the old lady.

'Poor thing,' murmured Ursula. She reached into her belt pouch, pulled out a little copper quadrans and gingerly placed it in the old woman's filthy palm.

A moment later she cried, 'Hey!' as the old woman gripped her wrist.

With strength surprising in someone so frail, the old woman pulled Ursula closer and gazed into her face with an alarming intensity.

'Hey!' cried Ursula again. 'Let me go!'

The old woman opened her mouth and let out a wordless wail. Tears began to streak her grimy cheeks. But she still would not release her grip.

Gartha bared her teeth and gave her distinctive wheezy growl.

This made the woman let go of Ursula, but she did not stop crying. Her lament was louder than ever.

Juba and the others came up, out of breath. 'What is it?' cried Juba. 'What's the matter?'

'Did she hurt you?' asked Doctor Jonathan.

'Did you hurt her?' asked Bouda.

'No!' said Ursula, rubbing her wrist.

When the old woman caught sight of Juba, she suddenly stopped wailing. She pointed at him, and then mimed rocking a baby in her arms.

Suddenly Ursula understood.

'Juba!' she gasped. 'It's Calpurnia's mother.'

'Whose mother?' asked Bouda.

'Calpurnia's!' cried Ursula. 'The woman who took baby Dora.' She turned to Juba. 'Remember the old lady who never spoke?'

'Dear gods!' whispered Juba.

The old beggar lady nodded vigorously and pointed at Ursula and then at Juba. Ursula remembered the silent lady being dignified, happy and well-dressed. Now the ragged neck of her stola was soaked with tears of anguish.

'Domina,' said Juba respectfully. 'Tell us, please. Where is your daughter?'

157

The woman made a stabbing motion into her belly. Then she shook her head.

'She's dead?' whispered Ursula.

The old woman nodded.

'What about your daughter's husband?' asked Ursula. 'He was so kind to us. Where is he?'

The old woman made a slicing motion across her neck.

'And your son?' asked Juba. 'He also helped us escape from Rome.'

Again the woman made the slicing motion. Her face was so contorted by anguish that it looked like a tragic mask.

'Soldiers?' whispered Juba. 'With white crests?'

The old lady nodded and Ursula cried, 'Juba, we have to help her!'

'Of course we do,' said Juba and helped Ursula pull the old lady to her feet. Her bones were as light as a bird's but her grip was as taut as a bowstring.

When they asked her name she shook her head and showed them her grey hair and let them call her Avia, which meant 'grandmother'.

They took Avia with them to the Peacock Tavern and sat her in the dappled shade beneath the grape arbour and gave her chickpea pancakes and honey-water, which Jonathan called 'hydromel'. The cheerful innkeeper patted Gartha's head and said he had two free rooms if they liked – one for the women and one for the men – so Jonathan paid him a sestertius.

After their pancakes, Ursula and Bouda took the old lady to a nearby bath-house. They spent almost an hour in the tepidarium using Bouda's fine-toothed ivory comb to remove the nits from the old lady's grey hair. Finally, in the caldarium, they oiled, steamed and scraped her.

When they got back to the Peacock Tavern they led Avia upstairs to one of the bedrooms overlooking the little courtyard and put her to sleep on a low bed. They took a siesta, too, for it was a hot afternoon and they were physically and emotionally exhausted.

When Avia woke at dusk, Jonathan prescribed morsels of roast cockerel and half a cup of hot peppered wine to balance her cold, watery humours. Lamps were already burning in the courtyard as the innkeeper brought out a spatchcock: a whole rooster plucked, cleaned, split in half and then pressed between iron plates over red-hot coals. It was accompanied by one of Ursula's favourite meals: a salad of chopped cabbage, barley and cheese in a dressing of oil and vinegar.

When nothing was left but bones, the innkeeper himself took away their plates and then returned with a platter of red apple slices with a sauce of garum, honey and mint drizzled over them. He was a big man about Jonathan's age with a double chin and kind eyes. 'Is that Calpurnia Firma's mother?' he said, nodding at the old lady. She had fallen asleep leaning against Doctor Jonathan's shoulder.

'Yes!' said Juba in surprise. 'You know her?'

'Of course,' said the innkeeper. 'Everybody in Ostia knows everybody else. I'll take her up to her room.'

He gathered old Avia in his arms and carried her upstairs as easily as if she were a toddler.

A short time later the innkeeper returned with a flask of wine.

'On the house,' he said.

'Thank you, but I don't drink wine,' said Jonathan. 'Do you have any more of that apple vinegar posca?'

'Of course.' The innkeeper took the wine away and returned with a jug of posca.

'You don't recognise me, do you?' The innkeeper was looking at Doctor Jonathan.

The doctor shook his head.

'I'm Porcius. I was kidnapped by slave traders when I was young. You and your friends sailed all the way to Rhodes to rescue me.'

'Porcius! The baker's son!' Doctor Jonathan stood up and gave his childhood friend a kiss of greeting. After he introduced Ursula and the others, he gestured around at the little courtyard with its grapevine arbour, glowing oil-lamps and splashing fountain. 'Is the Peacock Tavern yours now?'

Porcius nodded proudly.

'You've done well for yourself,' said the doctor.

'Thanks to you,' said Porcius.

'What do you mean?'

Porcius put his beaker of wine on the table and pulled up a chair next to Ursula. Gartha sat up and wagged her tail, and he stroked her head. 'Without you I would be a slave somewhere. Maybe even dead. Perhaps you don't realise' – the innkeeper's eyes welled with sudden tears – 'how much the people of this town love you. There is not a person in Ostia who was not helped in some way by you and your friends.' He wiped his tears, laughed and shook his head. 'Look at me: blubbing like a baby. Tell me, how are Flavia, Nubia and Lupus doing?'

'I will tell you,' said the doctor. 'But first tell me what has been happening here in Italy. Here in Ostia. I have been away for almost thirteen years.'

Porcius nodded and lowered his voice. 'Because we are alone here and because I trust you with my life, which I owe to you anyway, I will tell you the truth.'

'The truth?' said Jonathan. 'The truth about what?'

'The truth about Domitian, the monster who is now making people address him as master and god.'

Chapter Twenty-Nine
DOMINUS ET DEUS

Juba leaned forwards in order to hear.

Even though they were alone in the lamplit courtyard of the Peacock Tavern, the innkeeper Porcius had lowered his voice almost to a whisper.

'Did you know that last year Domitian ordered the execution of his cousin Flavius Clemens, whom he had made consul, and whose two sons he had chosen to be his successors?'

'Yes,' said Juba. 'That news reached us in Britannia.'

'And have you heard about the soothsayer?'

Juba and the others looked at each other and shook their heads.

'The Emperor's astrologer was a man named Ascletario—'

Doctor Jonathan sat up straight. 'I know him. He's the one who told me the date of Domitian's presumed assassination.'

Porcius nodded. 'It's the day after tomorrow. Correct?'

Jonathan knocked over his beaker of posca. 'How did you know that? Who told you?'

Porcius took a rag from his apron and mopped up the spill. 'Ascletario told many people recently,' he said.

'But that's dangerous!' cried Jonathan. 'Sharing the imperial horoscope is a crime punishable by death.'

'You should have been here to remind him of that,' said Porcius, tucking the rag back into his apron. 'Last week someone informed against Ascletario. Domitian called him into his private quarters – he hardly goes out these days – and angrily asked if Ascletario could predict his own death. Ascletario replied that he had seen his future long ago and that it was to be torn apart by dogs.'

'Oh, how horrible!' cried Ursula.

Porcius nodded. 'In order to prove that Ascletario could be wrong, Domitian commanded that he be executed immediately, and his remains burnt straightaway on a pyre outside the city gates. They had barely got the fire going when a sudden storm came rolling in and torrential rain doused the flames, leaving the body intact.' Porcius raised his eyebrows at them. 'Do you want to guess what happened next?'

'Dogs tore his body apart?' guessed Juba, with a nervous laugh.

'Exactly,' said Porcius, and they all gasped.

Porcius took a sip of wine and sat back so that his face was no longer illuminated by the oil-lamp. 'In the past year,' he said, 'there have been more signs and portents than anyone can remember. Jupiter's bolts have struck the capitol, the Temple of the Flavians and even Domitian's bedroom deep within his palace. In fact, there have been so many lightning strikes that some claim the Emperor looked up to the heavens, spread his arms and cried, "Strike me down if you dare!"'

Porcius leaned forward again, and the flickering lamplight made his face look mysterious and wise.

'Domitian worships Minerva above all others. But there is a rumour that she came to him in a dream last week and said she could not help him any more. She said that Jupiter had disarmed her. That is why our Princeps now lives in terror.'

Juba noticed Bouda was fingering the Minerva gem as she often did when she was worried or frightened.

Porcius took a thoughtful sip of wine and put down the cup. 'The Emperor believes everybody is plotting against him. He barely made an appearance at the races this week, even though his palace overlooks the racecourse. Now he is secluded in his private wing, which he calls the Domus Augustana. He only sees his child slaves, his closest ministers and his wife, Domitia. And they say she has gone away to one of their other palaces, the one at Alba.'

Ursula frowned. 'So it's true?' she said. 'Is he going to be assassinated the day after tomorrow?'

Porcius shrugged. 'Who knows? Time will tell.' The innkeeper drained his cup and stood. 'It's late,' he said. 'I'll let you sleep. If you need anything, don't hesitate to ask.' He took their empty plates and beakers back to his kitchen.

'Juba,' whispered Bouda, catching his hand. 'If the Emperor is going to be dead in a few days, why don't we just wait here? Then we can bring home your little sister after the Emperor is dead.'

Juba shook his head. 'I've thought of that,' he said. 'But whether Domitian dies at the fifth hour on the day after tomorrow or not, I know that there will be an attempt on that day and at that time. And if soldiers are involved then who knows what could happen to a little two-year-old bedroom slave if she got underfoot? They might even make a conscious decision to kill everyone in the Emperor's household. I've got to get her out before the assassins arrive. Also,' he said, 'I gave my word to the man who told me about Dora. I have one job to do, and I plan to do it.'

Chapter Thirty
REDEMPTIO

In the lamplit courtyard of the Peacock Tavern, Ursula was sitting at the table with the others, stroking Gartha's head and trying to help think of a way to rescue baby Dora. Her mind was like a juggler with half a dozen balls. There were so many different things to consider.

Gartha gave a big yawn. That reminded Ursula of another element: the old lady asleep in their room upstairs.

'What shall we do about Avia?' she asked everyone.

Juba nodded. 'It's not just Dora we need to save, but that poor old woman.'

Doctor Jonathan said, 'Maybe my mother could take her in. She and her friend Hephzibah used to take in beggars and cripples.'

'Your mother?' said Ursula. 'Where does she live?'

'Right here in Ostia,' he replied.

'Of course!' cried Juba. 'That's why the twins were coming back here: so Raven could meet his grandmother.'

The doctor nodded. 'According to Castor, she owns a lovely villa outside the town walls, not far from the synagogue. I've never even been there,' he added.

'Why haven't you been to see her?' cried Ursula.

'Yes,' said Bouda. 'Why aren't we staying with her?'

'For the same reason I'm travelling under the name of Prometheus. Like you, I am an enemy of the Emperor. I don't want her to suffer by being linked to me.'

Ursula sat up straight. 'Maybe the twins are there! I mean here! And Loquax . . . I wonder if he's still alive.'

'If he is then I hope they keep him caged up in a room with thick walls so nobody can hear him,' said Bouda.

Juba made the sign against evil and then said, 'Old Avia is my responsibility. I'm going to sell the Nereid amethyst to make sure she has a room somewhere.' He looked around the little courtyard. 'Maybe even here.'

'But it's your last gem!' cried Bouda. 'And why is Avia your responsibility anyway?'

'Because I let her daughter adopt Dora. It's my fault that Calpurnia Firma and her husband and brother are dead. Oh gods!' He lowered his head and tugged his curly hair with both hands.

'It's not your fault,' said Bouda fiercely. 'It's the Emperor's.'

'Bouda's right,' said Ursula. 'You mustn't blame yourself.' She closed her eyes and lifted her palms to the starry sky above the grape arbour. 'Dear Lord, please give us a ruler who is just and good!' She looked at them and sighed. 'Doctor Jonathan and I have been praying that God would change Domitian's heart and help him see the truth. But so far it's not working!'

'It appears not,' admitted Doctor Jonathan. 'But we mustn't give up praying.'

'Sometimes prayer isn't enough!' cried Juba. 'Sometimes people have to act!' He looked around at them and lowered his voice. 'It's time I told you the details of my mission. Back in Colonia, Trajan and the man called Tortor gave me instructions.

166

I'm supposed to meet a man who calls himself Maximus at the foot of the colossal equestrian statue of Domitian.'

'When?' asked Ursula.

'At noon on the Ides of September—'

'That was two days ago!' interrupted Doctor Jonathan.

'Or on any of the four days following,' Juba said. 'I have one more chance to meet him. If I miss the appointment tomorrow then I won't get in.'

'How will you recognise this Maximus?'

'I won't. He'll recognise me.'

'How?'

Juba shrugged. 'My looks are distinctive.' He closed his eyes and recited, '*An exotic youth of fourteen with nutmeg-coloured skin, sage-green eyes and curly black hair.*'

Ursula gaped. 'Exotic?'

'Who said that?' asked Bouda.

'Trajan. He told me that I had one small but crucial role in the whole plan: to remove the blade of a dagger hidden under the imperial pillow.'

'So he can't defend himself when the assassins come,' murmured Doctor Jonathan.

'Exactly,' said Juba. 'The only two people who have regular access to the Emperor's bedroom are his personal attendant – his cubicularius – and also a boy who tends his private shrine to Minerva. The cubicularius is a slave but the shrine attendant is a freeborn boy. I am to be the Emperor's new shrine attendant. My job will be to remove the blade of the dagger.'

'Why not the whole dagger?' asked Doctor Jonathan.

'Because he might notice if the whole dagger is missing, but as long as the handle is in the scabbard he won't know the blade is gone.'

'So you're going to replace another shrine attendant?' said Jonathan. 'Won't the Emperor be suspicious of a late replacement this close to the dreaded day?'

'No. Because the shrine attendants are freeborn, they only serve for a few months at a time. Trajan told Domitian he was sending a special boy, one of great devotion and exotic appearance. He'll be expecting me. If it's not an elaborate trap,' he added under his breath.

'What's the rest of the plan?' asked Bouda. 'Who's going to assassinate him after you remove the blade?'

'They didn't tell me. They said the fewer details I knew, the safer it would be for all involved. They just told me to remove the blade of the knife a few hours before noon on Domitian's deathday.'

'His *deathday*?' echoed Bouda.

Juba nodded. 'Thirteen days before the Kalends of October,' he recited. And then added, 'The day after tomorrow.'

Ursula shivered. 'It sounds very dangerous.'

'Yes,' said Juba. 'But at least I'll be there to protect Dora and maybe get her out if something goes wrong.'

'I wish I could help you,' said Ursula.

'Me, too,' murmured Bouda. 'So many things could go wrong.'

They all made the sign against evil.

Doctor Jonathan said, 'What if we could save your little sister before the attempt?'

'How?' said Juba.

'We could redeem her,' said the doctor.

'What does "redeem" mean?' asked Ursula.

'It's when you buy something back that was yours in the first place.'

Ursula frowned. 'How can that happen?'

'If something is stolen or someone is kidnapped and you pay the ransom,' said the doctor.

'But it was already yours!' Ursula protested. 'That's not fair.'

Jonathan raised an eyebrow at her. 'Nobody said life was fair.'

Juba shook his head. 'But what can we offer the richest, most powerful man in the world? He can have anything or anyone he wants.'

'Perhaps not,' said Doctor Jonathan.

Bouda looked at Juba. 'You always tell me that money can't buy you safety. Oh!' She sat up straight, her eyes wide.

'What?' they all cried.

'Last night I dreamt that Minerva stood before me.'

'Minerva came to you in a dream?' Juba leaned forwards.

'Yes. I've only just remembered. She said, *Whatever you have in mind, do it, for I will be with you.* I didn't understand it but I've just had an idea.'

'What?' They all leaned forwards.

Bouda told them.

Ursula stared at her in amazement and Juba said, 'You would do that?'

Bouda nodded. 'Sometimes if you put something on an altar, the gods return it to you.'

'*Wisdom calls from the highest place,*' quoted Doctor Jonathan.

'The only problem with your idea,' said Juba, 'is that I was told not to bring anything in, apart from what I'm wearing: an undertunic and sandals.'

'Nothing changes about your part of the plan,' said Bouda. 'But if I can sneak in and offer him something in exchange for Dora . . .'

'But how will you sneak in?' cried Ursula.

169

Bouda raised an eyebrow. 'I used to be a cutpurse. I have ways . . .'

'Actually,' said Juba, 'getting in might be the easiest part. Tortor did tell me one other thing about the plot. The rear entrance to the palace will be unguarded from the third to the sixth hour on the morning of the fatal day, presumably to allow the assassins to get in and out. But the palace is massive. It's like the maze of the Minotaur on three levels. Once you're in, you'll have to find your way to Domitian's bedchamber, right in the most protected part. That's the challenge.'

'I know something else we could give him in exchange for Dora,' said Ursula shyly. 'But my gift is not as good as Bouda's.'

'Tell us!' they all said.

She told them.

'That's a good idea, too,' said Juba slowly. 'I think what Bouda is offering is better. But maybe we could use both plans. Your gift would give Bouda an excuse to be in the Emperor's private quarters, especially if she's dressed as a slave.'

Ursula said. 'I know Bouda is brave but how will she find the Emperor's bedroom on her own? She's never been to Rome, much less the Emperor's palace.'

Bouda lifted her chin. 'What I need is a guide,' she said with a nervous laugh.

'I can't give you a guide,' said Juba, 'but I can give you a trail to follow. Do you remember the memory trick I taught you last winter for remembering the order of topics in your speech?'

Bouda tilted her head. 'Cicero's Method of Backgrounds? Where I imagine each topic in a specific part of a Roman house as I pass through it?'

'No, the other method that helps you remember items in a list.'

170

'The number-picture system!' cried Ursula. 'Where number one is a soldier standing at attention and you put him guarding the thing you want to remember!'

'That sounds clever,' said Doctor Jonathan to Juba. 'Did you devise it?'

'We came up with a list together,' said Juba.

Ursula raised her hand. 'Can I tell him?'

Juba smiled. 'It will be Bouda's task. Let her try?'

Bouda closed her eyes. 'Number two is a pair of twins standing next to each other, three is a trident, four is a wax tablet because of its four sides and five is a golden hand. Five fingers,' she added.

'I used them to memorise the Ten Commandments,' said Ursula, unable to contain her excitement. 'You can make them move and do funny things so they stick in your mind's eye.'

'Carry on,' said Juba to Bouda. 'What's number six?'

'A beetle because it has six legs. Number seven is a lyre because it has seven strings. Eight is an octopus, which I've never seen except drawn on a wax tablet. Nine are the Muses and ten is a cross with a man on it.'

Juba nodded. 'Excellent.' He took a breath. 'When Tortor was cutting into my scalp to mark the date, he told me ten landmarks to guide me to the Emperor's bedroom, starting from the place where a secret ramp emerges into the gardens of the palace. Then he asked me to say them back and I did because I used the number-object system we devised. Those ten steps will guide you to the centre of the maze.'

Bouda took a deep breath. 'Then I have everything I need to put my plan into practice.'

'I can help by praying for you,' offered Ursula. 'And by getting the gift to help you get in.'

'Good,' said Juba. He looked at the doctor. 'Doctor Jonathan? As our plan involves no bloodshed but only the rescue of Dora, will you help us?'

Ursula tugged on her teacher's cloak. 'Please, Doctor Jonathan?' she pleaded.

He closed his eyes and shook his head. 'We'll probably all die horribly but Flavia Gemina made me promise to look after you, so yes.' He sighed deeply. 'Yes, I will help you.'

Chapter Thirty-One
EQUUS

Bouda could hardly believe she was in Rome.

Rome! The Eternal City. The place she had always dreamt of visiting.

It was mid-morning of the following day, fourteen days before the Kalends of October. She and Juba were standing on a cobbled street at the northern foot of the Palatine Hill. The buildings rising up before her were made of creamy marble, peach-coloured plaster, red brick buttresses and orange-red roof tiles. A lofty aqueduct ran along one side of the hill.

'I don't see it,' Bouda said to Juba. She shaded her eyes against the bright autumn sun. 'Which one is his palace?'

'All of it,' said Juba. 'All those buildings on top of the hill are part of Domitian's palace.'

'All of it?' She stared in disbelief.

'Yes.' He pointed to the right. 'That part is called the Domus Flavia. It's the public part of the palace, where he receives visitors and gives dinner parties. Those buildings on the left form the Domus Augustana, which is private. There are also gardens, temples and even a school to train his servants. That's probably where they'll take me,' he said. 'It's called the Paedagogium and it's on the other side of the hill, overlooking the Circus Maximus.'

He turned his head to gaze at a house across a cobbled square. It had green double doors flanked by columns of purple marble. Although dwarfed by the buildings on the hill above them, it was still a mansion.

'Who lives there?' she asked.

'I don't know who lives there now,' he said. 'But it used to be our house.'

The memories must have been painful, for he was now holding her hand so hard that it hurt.

'Ow!' she said.

'Oh. Sorry.' He came out of his reverie and let go of her hand. 'Follow me,' he said and led the way across the cobbled street to a public fountain beneath one of the aqueduct arches. Behind the fountain was a single parasol pine surrounded by shrubs. At the foot of the tree was rich soil scattered with pine needles.

'Sometimes when I was little,' he said, 'I would come out here with one of the slaves who fetched water. This was my secret den.' He took her behind the tree and used a piece of bark to dig a small hole. He reached into the neck of his tunic and brought out the little statuette of Mercury that he always carried on him.

He held it reverently and prayed, 'Mercury, please protect us and guide us. If I come back to collect you I promise that one day you will take pride of place in my own household shrine with the Lares and Penates and other household gods.'

He placed the figurine in the hole, covered it over and sprinkled pine needles on it so that nobody could tell the earth had been dug up.

It was quiet in their hidden place there at the foot of the

trec. Bouda could hear the spatter of the fountain and slave-girls chattering. Somewhere a rooster crowed and above them the swifts and swallows were uttering their piercing cries.

Juba turned to her and stroked her hair back from her face. It was dark brown again and still damp from the walnut-shell dye Porcius had prepared early that morning. 'I hope that your patron goddess Minerva will stand beside my Mercury one day in our household shrine,' he said.

Bouda gazed into his beautiful grey-green eyes. 'That is my wish, too,' she said.

'What happened here that night two years ago was awful,' Juba whispered, 'but a good thing came out of it. The gods brought me to you in far-away Britannia. And if they are willing, you and I will make a home together with Dora and old Avia and Ursula, until she is old enough to marry.' He took her hands. 'And maybe one day with children of our own?'

She nodded. 'In the bath-house that first morning after the horrible storm at sea, Ursula asked me what I would carve on a gem to represent my heart's desire.'

He cocked his head at her, not understanding.

Bouda continued, 'She told me to close my eyes and let my heart show me a picture. So I did. In my mind's eye I saw a gem. It was a leaf-green oval with a picture of a tiny garden. There were trees, columns, a bubbling fountain, a bench and a statue in the middle. I've been thinking a lot about that picture. I think the trees stand for life and the columns for civilisation. Roman civilisation. The bubbling fountain symbolises refreshment. Because the bench is a seat for more than one person, it makes me think of two people at least, maybe more, so that stands for family. The inner garden is protected by the house around it,

175

and also by Minerva. For she was the goddess who brought me to you.'

He looked at her with brimming eyes. 'That is a beautiful desire. Do you know you can sum it all up in one word?'

She shook her head and looked at him in puzzlement. 'Which word?'

'Home,' he whispered. 'Your heart's desire is for a home.'

Chapter Thirty-Two
CRYPTA

Juba held Bouda's hand until the moment they saw the giant bronze horse. That was when he let go to make the sign against evil.

'It's as big as the Trojan horse!' breathed Bouda. 'Only made of bronze, not wood,' she added.

'Did I ever tell you,' said Juba, 'how on the night we escaped from Rome I pretended we were Trojans fleeing the Greeks?'

'Yes,' she said. 'So Fronto and Ursula wouldn't be frightened. You took all the responsibility yourself.' She kissed his cheek then pointed to the huge statue. 'The man riding the horse,' she whispered. 'Is that . . .?'

Juba nodded grimly. 'Domitian,' he said.

The lofty bronze rider faced east and on the open palm of his giant left hand stood Minerva, goddess of war and wisdom. She looked down into the forum and it seemed to Juba that she was looking at him.

He wondered if the goddess would approve or disapprove of what he was about to do.

He turned to Bouda. 'I have to go on my own now,' he whispered, pulling her back behind a column. 'Follow me at a distance to see which way we go. Be careful not to let yourself be seen. Can you do that?'

She gave him a wobbly smile. 'I was a cutpurse for more than five years. I can manage a bit of stealth.'

'Good. Trajan said the man called Maximus would take me through the entrance that will be unguarded tomorrow so I know where it is in case I need to escape after the assassination. Or in case it all goes wrong. If you're wearing the unbelted tunic of a slave you won't be stopped when you enter. Domitian's not afraid of women and children, just armed men. If anyone challenges you, just be confident and tell them you have a message for the Emperor.'

'So getting in will be easy,' she said. 'But finding my way to his bedroom will be the challenge.'

He nodded. 'But you remember the ten steps, don't you?'

'Yes. Eight is the one I keep forgetting.'

'What object represents eight?' he said patiently.

'The octopus,' she said and closed her eyes. 'It's the hardest one because I've never seen one in real life. Oh! I have it! I see an octopus rising out of water and wrapping its arms around an Amazon carrying a semi-circular shield, a pelta. So the Amazon fountain is number eight.'

'That's it!' he said. 'And if the gods are willing I'll be waiting for you there.'

She nodded, and kissed him.

He kissed her back fiercely; if anything went wrong, it might be the last time they would see each other.

Then he made his way out from the shadow of the colonnade and into the blaze of sunlight.

He picked his way through the milling crowds. Past the herald announcing a case, past a priest preparing for a noon sacrifice, past a poet proclaiming a rude epigram. Finally he reached the right hind foot of the gigantic horse. Only moments later, a man with a broad-brimmed travelling hat appeared beside him, and identified himself as Maximus.

'Juba?' he said in a low voice. 'Juba from Colonia?'

Juba nodded.

'Follow me.' He turned and led the way to a narrow, urine-smelling space between the horse's left rear hoof and the base of a statue of Vespasian. There, out of sight of any passers-by, he quickly examined the top of Juba's head. A moment later he gave a grunt of approval.

'Keep up!' was his next terse command. He wove between statue bases and columns to the Forum of Caesar, also known as the Roman Forum. Behind the temple of Castor and Pollux, and within view of the Temple of Vesta, was a steep cliff rising up.

This sheer side of the Palatine Hill was faced with brick arches that served as buttresses. The arched wall stopped the earth from crumbling and also formed a foundation for the buildings of the imperial palace high above.

Most of the arches were only shallow and filled in with brick. But one lofty arch was the entrance to a tunnel that pierced the cliff.

The base of this arch was flanked by columns and guarded by two white-crested soldiers, members of the Emperor's Praetorian Guard. As Juba and his guide came closer, he saw that the tunnel had a ramped floor wide enough to take a wagon.

'This is the rear entrance to the palace, where they usually bring deliveries,' said Maximus over his shoulder. 'Stay silent. Let me do the talking.'

'Salve, Maximus!' said one of the guards. 'Afraid I have to

search you, sir.' He looked Juba up and down. 'And also your
. . .' He trailed off and raised an eyebrow.

'He's the Emperor's, not mine,' said Maximus. 'A new shrine
attendant.'

The guard nodded, patted them both all over and even lifted
Juba's tunic. Finally he stepped back to his post. 'You may pass.'

The great vault reminded Juba of the tunnel to Naples which
his family had taken one year when the shore route was closed.
The tunnel burrowed through a mountain and cut a whole day
off their travel time. But his mother had hated it; she said it was
like going into Hades, so they had never used it again.

Like the Naples tunnel, this one had a lofty vaulted ceiling,
over thirty feet high. Unlike the Naples tunnel, the ramp went
up in gentle stages but with abrupt racecourse turns. The first
stage of the ramp took them past a side room full of crates and
barrels and the first about-face turn took them past a statue of
Aesculapius with a boy and a rooster. At this point the ramp was
only dimly illuminated by flickering torches and small windows.
Once they met two white-clad slaves coming down, a girl and a
boy not much younger than Juba. It was so dim he could barely
make out their features.

Finally, the light began to grow brighter. At the fifth turn
Juba saw the skyline of Rome up ahead, framed by an arched
opening at that end of the ramp. Presently the massive bronze
head of Domitian appeared in the archway and began to block
the view of Rome. It loomed higher and bigger with each step
they took.

It was a relief when the final turn of the ramp put the colossal
statue behind them and brought them into vast kitchen gardens.

Maximus led the way through a door in a brick wall
surrounding the gardens. Then they passed along several

colonnaded walkways in what were clearly the kitchen and workshop areas of the palace.

At this point they diverted from the route Juba had been given and for a moment he panicked.

Then the cheer of a quarter of a million Romans up ahead told Juba they were heading south for the slope that overlooked the Circus Maximus. He reckoned they were not going to the Emperor's bedroom but to the Paedagogium, the school for slaves and imperial attendants. His father had once pointed it out to him when they had gone as a family to the races.

'The Emperor's new shrine servant,' said Maximus to the white-haired slave who answered his scratch on a nondescript door. 'A gift from Trajan.'

'He's late.' The old slave scowled at Juba. 'And these are dangerous times. The Emperor expected him on the Ides and is about to interview other boys.'

Juba could tell by the expression on Maximus's face that he had not expected this.

'May the boy at least enter the trials?'

'Very well,' said the old man. 'Come in. Not you,' he said to Maximus. 'Just him.'

Juba swallowed hard. For their plan to work, he would have to pass some sort of test.

And he had no idea what it would be.

Chapter Thirty-Three
CUBICULARIUS

In addition to Juba, there were four other boys waiting in the apodyterium of the Paedagogium baths. He guessed they were aged between twelve and fifteen.

They were given an hour in a caldarium with scented oil and strigils. The afternoon sun made beams of gold in the steam rising from the hot plunge. Juba wondered if any of the others had been asked to disarm the Emperor, but he dared not ask.

Back in the changing rooms of the baths, an attendant gave each of them an Egyptian-style kilt to wear. These short linen loincloths had neither belt nor undergirding. No place to hide a dagger or phial of poison.

Slaves with tweezers and cosmetics worked briefly to enhance their looks. Juba's eyes were lined with black kohl and his eyelids painted with shimmery green malachite. Finally, each of them was given a small wooden name plaque to hang around their necks. Juba's label read *Hyacinthus*, after the mythical youth whose hair curled like the petals of a hyacinth.

A tall man with skin the colour of papyrus and receding black hair came into the room, followed by a blond boy. The tall man held a wax tablet and stylus and walked up and down, inspecting them carefully.

Finally he stood back and nodded. 'My name is Parthenius and I am the Emperor's chief steward. This' – he gestured to the blond boy beside him – 'is the Emperor's head cubicularius, his chief bedroom slave. His name is Satur.'

Juba stared at the boy whom Trajan had claimed was utterly loyal to Domitian.

Satur was a slender youth with silky blond hair, slanting eyes and lips stained pink. Like the other boys, he wore only a white linen loincloth. His torso was smooth and hairless.

'You are in competition,' continued Parthenius, 'to serve the most powerful man in the world, who is indeed like unto a god. Today one of you will be chosen to attend his private shrine to Minerva until the festival of Saturnalia. Whenever you are in the divine presence, you are to keep your eyes respectfully lowered and address him as *Dominus et Deus*, my master and my god. Do you understand?'

They all nodded.

'The test,' said Parthenius, 'will be one of loyalty and bravery. Follow me.'

Leaving the sunny rooms of the Paedagogium, Parthenius and pretty blond Satur led them through a maze of chilly marble corridors and stairs, moving deeper and lower as they went.

Finally they came into a large sunken courtyard with a splashing fountain at its centre. Four pairs of marble Amazons fighting bronze Greeks stood on four semi-circular islands around the sparkling jets of water. Juba recognised it as landmark eight, the Amazon fountain.

Two levels of the palace rose up around this sunken garden and the blue sky was visible up above them. Parthenius made them stand against a marble wall near double doors of oak. He had lined them up in order of height and Juba was third. The late afternoon sun bathed them with a golden light that made them blink.

Although the September sun was warm, the marble wall behind them was cold and smooth against their backs; Juba was aware of the boy on his left shivering.

Suddenly the guards stood to attention as a tall man with dark curly hair emerged from one of the corridors.

He held a bow in his left hand and was dictating something to a scribe. Another attendant held a quiver full of arrows.

The man with the dark hair finished dictating and turned to them. 'Greetings, dear boys! Yes, it is I! Your lord and god, Titus Flavius Caesar Domitianus Augustus.'

For the first time, Juba saw his enemy in the flesh.

The Emperor did not look like a monster. He was a slightly overweight middle-aged man with a double chin, pink cheeks and curly black hair.

Juba felt almost disappointed. This was the person he had feared for two years? Then he reminded himself that this ordinary-looking man was the cause of his parents' death.

Domitian turned to the tallest of the boys entering the trials, a pretty youth with wavy brown hair almost touching his tanned shoulders.

'Ganymede,' said the Emperor, peering at the youth's name tag. 'Step forward, Ganymede.'

Ganymede stepped forward and promptly vomited on to the marble floor.

'Oh dear,' said Domitian, shaking his head. 'We can't have vomit in the shrine of Minerva. Take him away.'

A slave in a white tunic hurried the trembling youth away. Another slave appeared with a bucket and sponge to mop up the puddle.

'Step forward, Zephyrus,' said the Emperor.

Zephyrus stepped forward. A slender boy with curly yellow hair, blue eyes and skin the colour of thick cream. He did not vomit on the floor, but Juba could see him shivering.

'Zephyrus, what would you do for your Emperor?'

'Anything, O lord and god,' said Zephyrus in a shaky voice.

'Would you stand in front of that oak door and spread your fingers and allow me to shoot an arrow between your forefinger and thumb?'

'What?' said Zephyrus, his creamy skin turning a ghastly chalk colour.

'I am an excellent shot,' said the Emperor, notching an arrow on its string.

Zephyrus fainted.

Domitian rolled his eyes. 'Take him away!' he said and turned to squint at Juba's label. 'Hyacinthus!' he cried. 'What would you do for me, your master and god?'

Juba's heart was thudding, but the image of his dead parents filled him with anger. And that gave him courage. 'I would die for you, O master and god!' he cried. He stepped over to the oak doors and held out his right hand, the fingers spread wide. By pressing the back of his hand to the wood, he was able to keep it still.

If the arrow struck him, he reasoned, it was no more than he deserved for abandoning his baby sister. And if it missed . . .

Thunk! Domitian's arrow buried itself harmlessly in the wood between his thumb and forefinger.

At this, the next boy fainted. The bucket slave returned just in time to help Parthenius revive him and help him out of the room.

That left Juba with only one rival, a boy with jet-black skin and golden eyes whose name tag read *Memnon*.

Satur handed Domitian another arrow and the Emperor notched it in his bowstring. Before he could address the final candidate, Memnon ran out of the room after Parthenius, the slaves and the boys.

Juba felt a surge of courage; the gods were with him!

'Here is my other hand, O master and god!' he cried, and splayed the fingers of his left hand, pressing them hard against the wooden door.

'No need,' said Domitian with an approving nod. 'You have proved yourself brave and loyal. And besides, you are the only one standing. You will have the honour of tending the Lares and the goddess Minerva in my bedroom shrine.' As he turned to leave he smiled at Satur. 'Show our new shrine attendant the way to my bedroom. I will join you soon.'

Chapter Thirty-Four
LARARIUM

'This is the Emperor's bedroom,' said Satur a short time later. Juba followed the pretty blond slave-boy into a luxurious room of white and gold. Pearly light from a roof of glass bricks showed a large canopied bed in its centre. Juba looked around eagerly, not admiring the beautiful surroundings, but hoping to see his little sister for the first time in two years.

Instead of his little sister, he saw himself entering the room.

The walls were made of the same reflective marble as some of the corridors.

Drawn as if by sorcery, Juba walked to the mirrored wall to look at himself and saw his own jaw drop. The smoky eyeliner and shimmery green eyeshadow made him look like a female version of himself.

'Come,' said Satur, from a corner of the room near the head of Domitian's bed, where there was a doorway to a small niche-room. 'Let me show you where you will live and sleep: here in the Emperor's personal lararium.'

The octagonal room was narrow but lofty. A citrus-wood chest was topped by a marble model of the Temple of Minerva. In it stood two fine Lares, statuettes of dancing youths wearing fluttering tunics and holding sacred vessels. One was made of silver and the other of gold. These were flanked by no fewer than seven statuettes of Minerva, each a different size and material. Juba noticed two Greek vases – one a flat cup and one a jug – also depicting the goddess.

'Do you know how to tend the shrine?' Satur asked.

Juba pointed at a small cone of incense burning on the steps of the miniature temple. 'Keep the incense burning?'

'That's all there is to it,' said Satur. He pointed to a rolled-up rush mat against the wall. 'You will even sleep in here so that no harm can come to the images. Keep them clean and polished. And watch for any portents. Any changes in their expressions or cryptic pronouncements.'

'They talk?' said Juba in astonishment.

'Not so far. But she did come to him in a dream last week.'

Juba feigned ignorance. 'Minerva appeared to him?'

'Yes.' Although they were alone, Satur lowered his voice and leaned so close that Juba could smell his perfumed hair. 'She told him that she could no longer be his protector. He spent half the morning in here, weeping and pleading, and had the previous shrine boy scourged on the grounds that he had not tended the goddess with enough devotion.'

Juba swallowed hard. 'He had the previous boy whipped?'

Satur nodded. 'Until his back was in ribbons.'

Suddenly, without warning, he clasped Juba's face in both hands and made him bow his head. Juba's heart was racing but he forced himself not to panic.

What was Satur doing?

Then Juba felt the slave's deft fingers parting the curls on his head.

And he knew what Satur was after.

Juba tried to writhe away, but it was too late.

188

The Emperor's most trusted body slave had seen the tattoo on his scalp: *XIII K Oct Dom occ.*

It meant: *Thirteen days before the Kalends of October, Domitian will die.*

Juba had carried that prophetic date on his scalp for over three months. And now it had been discovered, less than twenty-four hours before that fateful day dawned.

'Don't look so terrified,' said Satur. 'I hate him more than anyone.'

Juba almost fainted with relief. The beautiful cubicularius had fooled everyone into believing he was completely loyal to Domitian.

'I'm sure you can guess my reasons,' said Satur. 'What are yours?'

Juba took a breath to still his racing heart, then confessed everything. 'He made my parents kill themselves, confiscated our wealth and turned me and my siblings into fugitives. I had to leave my baby sister behind,' he added. 'I thought she was safe but Domitian had her foster parents executed and enslaved her. Now she has to empty his chamber pot even though she is not yet three years old.'

Satur's blue eyes opened wide. 'You're Dora's brother!'

Hope leapt in Juba's heart. 'Yes! Is she all right? Is she still alive?'

Satur laughed. 'Don't worry; she's one of his favourites. She hasn't had to empty the chamber pot in a while. You'll probably see her later.'

The wave of relief was so great that Juba almost passed out. He rested a hand on the marble wall to steady himself.

'When can I take Dora home?' he asked Satur. 'When are you going to—'

'Shhh!' Satur pressed his forefinger to Juba's lips. 'He's coming!' Satur grabbed Juba's hand again and pulled him out of the shrine and back into the bedroom.

A moment later someone came in. At first, Juba couldn't see properly because the big bed with its gold columns and gauzy white canopy was in his way.

But when the Emperor emerged from behind it and came towards them, Juba saw that he was carrying a child.

It was a little girl with brown skin and silky black curls. She was laughing and waving chubby arms.

Once again, Juba felt his knees wobble and had to stop himself from falling.

'Ah,' murmured Satur, looking from the little girl to Juba and back. 'Now I see it clearly.'

As Domitian came closer, the toddler in his arms turned to look at Juba. The expression in her golden brown eyes was not recognition, merely curiosity.

For little Dora had not seen her brother Juba in over two years.

Chapter Thirty-Five
PRECES

The next day, two hours after dawn, Bouda cautiously emerged from the porch of the Temple of Minerva where she had spent a sleepless night.

Barefoot and dressed only in her newly hemmed and bleached linen undertunic, she hoped she would blend in with the other slaves at the Domus Augustana. Her long sleeves hid the little folding knife she had owned since the age of five and the high neck of the undertunic showed only the leather thong of the Minerva gem.

The sun was pushing golden fingers of light between columns and statues as she made her way gingerly out of the Forum Transitorium and past the base of the massive horse with his loathsome rider. Retracing her steps from the day before, when she had followed Juba, Bouda went past the circular Temple of Vesta to the back of the Temple of Castor and Pollux. The feel of cool paving stones beneath the bare soles of her feet brought back memories of her days in Tyranus's gang.

She was almost in view of the ramp's lofty arch when she heard a hiss from above. 'Bouda!'

Looking up, she saw Ursula's dark face peering down at her from between branches of a parasol pine.

'Wait there! I'm coming down!' Ursula dangled for a moment from one arm, then landed as lightly as could be expected for a healthy eleven-year-old girl.

They hugged each other and then Ursula stepped back and looked Bouda up and down.

'Good!' she said. 'Doctor Jonathan and I have seen some of the imperial slaves coming and going. We were worried because your tunic was too long and not white enough. How did you fix it?'

'I cut off the bottom with my wrist-knife and used my bone hairpin needle to make a new hem. Then I took it to a fuller's in the Subura to get it bleached. It's still damp and smells a bit,' added Bouda, sniffing her own sleeve, 'and it cost all my money and my signet ring.'

'Oh Bouda! Your precious ring!'

Bouda shrugged. 'Juba told me it was brass and glass, not gold and carnelian,' she confessed. 'I think Tyranus made up the story about me being Boudica's great-granddaughter.' Her stomach growled.

'Have you had anything to eat today?'

Bouda shook her head. 'Nothing today or yesterday.'

'Have this.' Ursula reached down the front of her tunic and brought out a heel of rye bread.

'Don't you want it?'

'No,' said Ursula. 'Doctor Jonathan and I are fasting and praying for you today. Come on!' she added over her shoulder. 'He's waiting over there with Gartha.'

Bouda followed her to the colonnade at the back of the Temple of Castor and Pollux. Against one wall Doctor Jonathan sat cross-legged, his head bent over a papyrus scroll. He was flanked by Gartha on one side and a covered birdcage on the other.

'You got Loquax!' cried Bouda.

Jonathan looked up, smiled and rose to greet her.

'We went to my mother's house in Ostia yesterday,' he said. 'We hid in the woods and saw the twins coming back from the synagogue. As I suspected, they are staying with her. They agreed to keep our visit a secret.'

'And they secretly smuggled out Loquax in his cage without Jonathan's mother knowing,' added Ursula. 'And here he is!'

'Your mother still doesn't know you're here in Italy?' asked Bouda.

'No,' said the doctor. 'But the twins told us she is well.'

Bouda nodded and gazed around. 'Where is everyone? I thought it would be busier.'

'Today is the penultimate day of a festival to Jupiter,' said Doctor Jonathan. 'A quarter of Rome's population are at the races.'

From somewhere in the forum came the faint voice of the herald confirming that it was the third hour of the ninth day of the Ludi Romani.

'Look!' Ursula gripped Bouda's arm and pointed. 'It's happening.'

Bouda turned. Between columns she could just make out the tall but narrow entrance in the sheer side of the Palatine Hill. Two soldiers were disappearing up the ramp.

Nobody took their place.

The back entrance of the Palatine Hill lay unguarded.

Bouda felt slightly sick. Everything seemed to be happening just as Juba had said, but the bite of bread she had eaten lay like a pebble in her stomach.

Doctor Jonathan grasped her shoulders. 'Bouda, you don't have to do this, you know.'

'Yes, I do. I can't leave Juba there alone. I have to help him save Dora.'

'Very well.' His hands were firm and she could feel their warmth through the thin sleeves of her tunic. 'Ursula and I will wait for you here,' he whispered. 'We're both fasting and we will pray without ceasing.'

Bouda nodded and turned towards the entrance of the ramp.

'Don't forget Loquax!' hissed Ursula. She held out the covered birdcage.

Bouda gave Ursula a quick hug and allowed Jonathan to rest his hand briefly on her head and utter a prayer of protection.

Then, carrying the covered birdcage, she went out from between the columns, down three steps and across the open space.

When Bouda reached the lofty, unguarded entrance to the imperial ramp she glanced quickly around. Then she carefully stepped over the marble threshold with her right foot first. She braced herself for a soldier's hand to clamp down on her shoulder but nothing happened.

She started walking up the broad ramp. It was like going into the underworld. Only instead of going down, she was going up.

Chapter Thirty-Six
PHENGITES

Bouda found her way to the Emperor by using the number-object memory system that Juba had taught her.

Two was represented by a mental image of the twins, Castor and his brother Raven, bowing and sweeping their arms forward to show her a view over Rome. As she rounded the sharp curve bringing her on to the sixth ramp, she saw the vista of Rome, with Domitian's giant bronze statue dominating the foreground.

Three was a trident. Immediately she remembered the image she had made: a man using a trident instead of a hoe to dig holes for vegetables. That link told her that her third landmark was the kitchen garden. As she turned her back on the view of Rome and mounted the seventh and final ramp, she came out into the open air and saw rows and rows of vegetables along with vines and fruit trees. It was much bigger than she had imagined but it was unmistakably a garden.

Juba had told her always to head southeast, towards the sun, so she went along a path by a brick wall and looked for the next item on her list.

Four was a wax tablet with four sides. In her mind she had imagined the tablet in the hand of a naked nymph. Sure enough, there was a niche with a marble statue of a naked nymph, pale against a backdrop of dark green ivy.

As she headed for the niche, she felt a fluttering in the cage in her hand; Loquax had been covered for some time and was getting restless, but she did not dare take away the cloth. Up ahead and to her right, two white-clad slave-boys were raking dead leaves from between pear trees. She kept her head down and let her newly dyed brown hair screen her face, praying that she looked like just another slave returning from an errand. The scratching of their rakes stopped as they looked at her, but a moment later they resumed.

She moved purposefully to the niche with the nymph.

There, hidden behind dangling ivy, was a secret door for slaves. A huge cheer rose up as she opened it, making her jump. *It's only the crowds in the Circus Maximus*, she told herself, and she took a deep breath.

Now she was in the public part of the palace and saw huge marble buildings rising up before her: a massive basilica where the Emperor acted as judge, his audience hall for when he received important guests and a giant lararium with life-sized statues of the Emperor's ancestors and protective gods.

But the next landmark on her list was none of those.

Five was the golden hand. In her mind she had made a picture of a giant gold hand washing itself in jets of water shooting up in a big eight-sided fountain. The sound of water drew her to a massive peristyle courtyard with the biggest fountain she had ever seen at its centre. She stared open-mouthed as the jets of the octagonal fountain rose up and fell in a dozen different combinations until Loquax's fluttering once again reminded her of her mission.

Six was a six-legged beetle. It represented another hidden

slave door, one which would take her into the private part of Domitian's palace. In her mind's eye, she had made the beetle huge and set it to fighting Hercules. Scanning the massive courtyard, she spotted a painted marble statue of Hercules in the southeast corner, and behind it a nondescript door.

When she reached it, she pushed the door to find a narrow, dark corridor. As her bare feet padded along the earthen floor she tried to remember the seventh item on her list.

Seven was represented by a seven-stringed lyre. In her mind she had replaced the strings with red-and-blue columns, for her seventh landmark was a colonnade.

As she came out of the dark corridor into the private part of the palace she saw the expected red-and-blue columns. They surrounded the balcony of a sunken courtyard. Suddenly the sound of hobnail boots on marble warned her of patrolling guards. Just in time, she shrank back into the corridor and pressed herself against the plaster wall as they passed.

Bouda waited a long time. At last she cautiously set off along the walkway, heading southeast with the red-based blue columns on her left and a marble-faced wall on her right. She tried to remember the next landmark.

Number eight.

She always forgot that one.

And it didn't help that another slave had silently fallen into step beside her.

Letting her eyes slide right, Bouda saw it was a dark-haired girl of about her own age wearing an almost identical tunic. The poor creature was trapped in some kind of room behind the faintly veined transparent stone of the wall.

Bouda stopped to look at the girl and the girl also stopped to look back at her. Dark eyebrows, dull brown hair, pale eyes in a face full of freckles. Pretty in a feral kind of way. But her chin was too sharp, her eyes too wary. Like Bouda, the girl held a covered birdcage.

That was when Bouda understood.

The girl was her.

It was her own reflection in some kind of polished marble. Once or twice before she had seen her face dimly in a mirror, a small disc of polished bronze.

Now she could see her whole body clearly: the dyed brown hair, the slender bare feet, the slightly uneven hem of her newly shortened linen undertunic, the tips of her fingers just peeping out from the too-long sleeves. The thong of the Minerva gem around her neck.

And that face. Her face.

She was surprised at how pretty it was, even with all those freckles.

But there was something hunted about her expression. She looked like a thief.

Was it the eyes? Were they too narrow? She tried opening them a little wider.

That only made her look like a thief caught in the act.

She thought of Bircha, with her innocent blue eyes and slightly open mouth. Bouda tried to imitate her friend's expression of innocent surprise. Eyes wide, eyebrows slightly raised, lips parted in a half smile for happiness or shaping an 'O' for surprise.

There. That was better. Now she looked innocent and lost. It had been a long time since she had put on the mask Tyranus first taught her to wear on the docks of Londinium.

Turning away from her reflection and looking down to the left again, she noticed a fountain at the centre of the courtyard.

It had four islands, each in the shape of a pelta, an Amazon's shield. That was when she remembered her image of an octopus grappling with an Amazon. This was her next landmark. And there were the stairs leading down to it.

Down she went, deeper into the heart of the palace.

When she emerged into the large fountain courtyard she stopped in her tracks.

A man with dark, curly hair sat on the marble lip of the fountain. He was dressed simply in white. His head was down and his shoulders were shaking.

At first Bouda thought he was another slave. Then she saw his hands. They were clean and manicured with a ring on every finger, and on some two rings.

It could only be the Emperor Domitian.

The most feared man in the Roman Empire.

Alone and unprotected.

This was a gift from the gods, too good to be true.

Bouda flicked out the blade of her wrist-knife and moved towards the Emperor on silent bare feet.

Chapter Thirty-Seven
MISERICORDIA

B ouda moved into the sunken courtyard, a covered wicker birdcage in her left hand and a razor-sharp penknife in her right.

With only a few steps and a swipe she could slash his loathsome throat.

She had done it before.

Killed before.

So why were her knees trembling and her teeth chattering?

Maybe because this time there was no anger. No fear.

That other time – when she was nine years old and the man on top had been trying to squash her – she had acted out of instinct, slashing blindly.

And her sharp little knife had opened a vein in his neck.

She could still remember the feel of the blood as it covered her, warm and sticky. She could still hear his squeals of surprise. Like a pig being slaughtered.

She had not allowed herself to think of that in years, but now she could not stop remembering.

Her knees gave way and she found herself on the cold marble at his feet. The birdcage rolled on the ground and the cloth fell off.

'*Ave, Domitian!*' cried Loquax, reciting the first words he had been taught.

'By Minerva!' cried the Emperor. 'Who are you? Are you one of my slaves?'

Bouda sucked in air and tried to still her thundering heart. She seemed to hear a voice in her head. *Go back to your original plan*, said the voice. Juba's voice. Calm and steady.

Keeping her knife open but hidden, she looked up at the Emperor Domitian.

He had been weeping.

His eyes were still swollen.

He was human.

She knew she would not have the courage to kill him now, so she put back the blade as she stood.

'I am not one of your slaves,' she said. 'But you were right to call out to Minerva, for the goddess herself sent me with a gift and a message.'

Bouda picked up Loquax's cage and set it on the marble-paved floor at his feet.

'*Ave, Domitian!*' said Loquax again. And then, '*Carpe diem!*'

The Emperor picked up the cage and peered at the bird inside.

'Titus!' A smile spread across his face. 'You found Titus!'

'You named a bird after your older brother?'

'Yes!' He opened the door of the cage.

'*What ARE you doing?*' Loquax flew out and settled on the head of a marble Amazon behind Domitian.

'Where did you find him? Dear Titus! How I missed your daily greetings. Say "*Ave, Domitian!*"'

Loquax tipped his head on one side. But instead of greeting the Emperor he relayed a different message.

201

'*Cave Domitian!*' he said.

The Emperor's face crumpled and he began to cry again. 'They all hate me!' he said. 'Even Titus.' He slumped back down on to the fountain edge. 'Nobody loves me,' he sobbed. 'Nobody has ever loved me. Only Phyllis, my old nurse.'

'At least you had one person to love you when you were little,' said Bouda after a moment. 'I had nobody. I never even knew my mother.'

'I didn't know my mother, either,' he said.

With his dark hair, pink cheeks and long eyelashes, he reminded her of her old gang boss, Tyranus. Despite herself, she felt her heart softening towards him.

'When I was a boy,' he said, 'I used to pretend that Minerva was my real mother.'

Bouda nodded, then frowned as something occurred to her. 'How could Minerva have been your mother? She is a virgin goddess.'

'Exactly! She was the best kind of mother!' He looked at her with swimming eyes. 'One who did not bear children but chose to foster. But even she has abandoned me now.' He began to sob again.

'No she hasn't,' said Bouda with as much confidence as she could muster. 'Minerva is calling you to the highest good. She sent me to test you.'

Bouda used her left hand to pull out the Minerva gem on its greasy thong. 'See?

'The Minerva of Augustus!' He wiped his eyes with his sleeve and blinked at her. 'Where did you get that? Who are you?'

'I am just a beggar and cutpurse from Britannia. I am not important. I am an emissary of Minerva.'

He reached for the gem.

'Wait!' She dropped the gem back inside her neckline and held up her left hand, palm first. 'If you seize Minerva, then she will turn against you. She must come to you. And she will, but you must listen.'

He withdrew his hand. 'I'm listening,' he said, his brown eyes as wide as a child's.

Bouda nodded and began the story she had concocted of truth and lies. 'Two years ago in Londinium,' she said, 'I stole this gem from a boy fresh off the boat from Rome. For a year I was happy. I never got sick and never went hungry. Then one night almost a year ago, the goddess Minerva appeared to me in a dream.'

'Yes!' The Emperor leaned forward eagerly. 'She does that sometimes. Go on!'

'The goddess told me to go to Rome and give this gem to the Emperor, as a sign that she would protect him after all. She told me that she was going to test you. To make sure you were still loyal, even if she withdrew her protection.'

'Yes!' Tears glistened on his thick eyelashes. 'I *am* loyal. I worship only Minerva! The colossal statue of me holds her image. I built a temple to her in my new forum. I have nine images of her in my personal shrine and I sacrifice to her on all of her feast days. What more can she ask?'

'She told me that you must prove you love her by giving up something precious.'

'Name it!' he cried. 'What does she want? If it is in my power I will give it!'

'In my dream the goddess showed me an eagle holding a little brown-skinned girl in his talons. The eagle was you! As I put the gem around the eagle's neck, the eagle put the little girl into my arms.'

Domitian frowned, making a dusting of face powder crease on his forehead. 'Brown skin?'

Bouda nodded. 'The colour of nutmeg. Or oak. The same colour as the boy from whom I originally stole it.'

'Of course!' The Emperor jumped to his feet. 'Satur!' he called and at once a slave appeared from behind a column of the peristyle.

Bouda stifled a gasp. The slave had been hiding there all the time! Who knew how many other slaves or soldiers were lurking around here?

'Yes, O lord and god?' said Satur. He wore only a loincloth and was one of the most beautiful boys Bouda had ever seen, almost as beautiful as the twins.

'Fetch little Dora!' commanded Domitian. 'And bring her to my bedroom.'

As the slave-boy hurried out of the garden, Domitian beckoned Bouda. 'Come to my bedroom,' he said. 'I have something to show you.'

Bouda swallowed hard.

Her plan was working, but she seemed to hear Tyranus's voice from many years before: *You know what Domitian does to little girls? He does horrible things. And then he eats them.*

Her senses told her that the Emperor was not a monster, but her knees were trembling as she followed him to his inmost lair.

Chapter Thirty-Eight
PERSONA

As Bouda followed the Emperor along another wall of reflective marble, she saw him cast quick glances at himself. After the first look he sucked in his belly and pulled back his shoulders. After another he adjusted the curly dark hair on his head. For the first time Bouda realised it was a wig.

Turning right, he led her along a corridor with smooth plaster walls painted to look like buildings in a garden. Purple columns marbled with gold were so skilfully painted that they seemed to pop out of the wall. They framed painted scenes of buildings, colonnades, urns, plants, trees, arched windows and more columns. A strange mental image of the nine Muses painting a wall confirmed that this was number nine on her list.

As the Emperor stopped before a life-sized fresco of double doors, she saw a mental image of a crucifix – for the Roman numeral X – in front of a painted doorway. Her imagination had nailed an actor's mask to the cross and, sure enough, above the painted door was a painted actor's mask, white-bearded and grinning horribly to keep away evil.

She had reached her goal, the tenth and final item on her list: the Emperor's bedroom.

The door was painted like all the others, but when Domitian

pushed, it swung open to reveal a secret room. It was a clever double trick: a fresco painted to look like a door that was in fact an actual door.

Stepping into his bedroom was like stepping into a pearly cube. In the centre of the room stood a feather bed with a creamy bedspread. Slender gold columns at each of the four corners held a canopy of gauzy white linen. The floor was marble veined with gold and spread with white and cream carpets. The reflective wall opposite showed her wide eyes and open mouth as she followed him into the room.

'I want to show you the lovely face of Minerva as foster mother,' said Domitian.

He led her into a dimly lit octagonal room smelling of frankincense and candles.

Kneeling at the foot of a shrine to Minerva with his back to them was a half-naked slave-boy. He had just lit a cone of incense that sent a ribbon of sweet-smelling smoke up to the coffered ceiling. Like Juba, he had brown skin and silky black curls.

As he stood and turned to face them, she realised it *was* Juba.

His face remained as blank as a mask.

'Pass me that kylix, boy,' said Domitian.

With a small bow, Juba took a flat banqueting cup from the shrine and offered it to the Emperor.

'See the look of love in her eyes?' Domitian was showing the cup to Bouda. 'The tenderness?'

Bouda dutifully took the cup in her left hand and studied its outside. The ceramic surface showed the goddess with her arms outstretched towards a toddler. Minerva's profile was indeed beautiful, and her expression full of love.

Bouda let her gaze slide sideways to look at Domitian.

Up close he looked much older than he had at first sight. Heavy powder on his face did not quite hide tiny red veins on his puffy cheeks or the scabby wart on his forehead. His breath was rancid. She could see a vein throbbing in his thick neck. She remembered that he was a man who casually executed people, even his close family members. Like Tyranus, he only cared for himself.

The cup was in her left hand but her right was free. Almost in a dream, she flicked open her penknife. Just one slash . . .

She allowed herself a quick glance at Juba, but his eyes were down and his jaw clenched as he tried to hide his emotions.

Bouda adjusted her grip on the knife and took a deep breath.

'*Tata!*' All three of them turned at the sound of footsteps. A little dusky-skinned girl in a snow-white tunic had come into the small room. '*Tata!* Daddy!' she cried again and lifted her chubby arms to Domitian.

'Dora!' The Emperor lifted the toddler into his arms. 'My little nutmeg. Give your Princeps a kiss.' Obediently she kissed his wet red lips.

Bouda felt sick, but she mastered her emotions and remembered her original plan. 'That's her!' she cried, handing the kylix back to Juba. 'That is the little girl I saw in my dream!'

Domitian nodded and stroked the toddler's curly hair. 'She is currently the dearest thing in my life,' he said. 'Apart from my old nursemaid, Phyllis, Dora is the only creature in this whole city who truly loves me.'

Bouda gave Juba a quick glance and then spoke to the Emperor.

'Sometimes the gods ask us to give up the thing we want most,' she said softly, 'just so they can give it back. Give her to me and in return receive the Minerva of Augustus, along with her protection.'

Bouda undid the clasp at the back of her neck and held out the Minerva gem on its leather thong.

Reluctantly, Domitian handed over little Dora.

With a silent prayer of thanks, Bouda handed him the gem and took Dora in her arms.

Domitian suddenly turned his back to Juba. 'Put it on me, boy,' he commanded. And to Bouda, he said, 'Where will you take little Dora?'

Bouda shifted the heavy toddler on to her left hip.

'I will take her to the Temple of Minerva which you yourself built,' she lied. 'The priestesses will look after her.'

'Do you think they will ever return her to me?'

'It is up to Minerva,' said Bouda. 'I am only her servant.' She edged out of the octagonal room into the brighter light of his bedroom.

'Your divine neck is too muscular, O lord and god,' came Juba's voice. 'It needs a longer thong, or better yet, a gold chain.'

'Very well,' said Domitian. 'Ask Satur or one of the slaves to see to it as soon as possible.' He came out of the octagonal shrine room.

'Go!' he said to Bouda. 'Take Dora before I weaken and change my mind. Goodbye, dear one.' As the Emperor came close to kiss Dora, Bouda saw Juba over his shoulder.

He gave her a wobbly smile and mouthed the words, *I love you.*

I love you, too, said her lips without making a sound.

As soon as Domitian stepped back, she shifted Dora to her right hip and hurried out of the bedroom. As she turned left into the painted corridor, she collided with a blond man in a red tunic and jostled his bandaged left arm. 'I'm sorry!' she cried. 'Did I hurt you?' She lightly touched the injured arm.

He rounded on her with such fury that Dora whimpered and buried her face in Bouda's neck.

'I'm fine,' the man hissed. 'Get out!'

Behind him stood a tall man with sallow skin and greasy, thinning black hair.

'I suggest you take his advice,' said the taller man.

'Want Tata!' cried baby Dora, stretching her arms back towards the Emperor's bedroom as the two men disappeared inside.

'Shhh!' whispered Bouda, kissing Dora's smooth cheek.

'WANT TATA!' cried Dora, squirming to get down.

Bouda put down the little girl and crouched before her. 'Dora!' she said. 'Do you like puppies?'

Dora put her thumb in her mouth and nodded.

'Would you like to meet the biggest puppy in the world?'

Dora pondered this for a moment and then nodded. 'Puppy!' she said. 'Want big puppy!'

'Good.' Bouda took the little girl's hand. Then she looked around in confusion, suddenly panicked. She was in the now empty painted corridor, number nine on her list, crowded with imaginary Muses. What was number eight again?

Octopus! Amazon. The Amazon fountain. To her left. The way she had come.

Dora knew, too, for she had already started along the corridor.

Heart thudding, Bouda followed. They might just get away.

That was when the screaming started.

Chapter Thirty-Nine
CLADES

The moment Bouda carried Dora out of the Emperor's bedroom, Juba breathed a sigh of relief and sank to his knees before the shrine of the goddess. 'Thank you, Minerva,' he whispered. 'Please guide them safely back out. And tell me what to do. Should I follow them now? Or wait long enough to make sure they're safely away?'

'Satur!' came Domitian's voice. He was still in the bedroom, but out of Juba's sightline.

'Yes, O lord and god?' Juba heard Satur reply.

'What time is it? Is it the fifth hour yet?'

'An hour past,' lied Satur. 'Can't you tell? It's noon.'

'Praise Jupiter, Juno and especially Minerva!' cried Domitian. 'The hour of danger has passed! Minerva did not abandon me after all. Has that girl gone? Has she taken my little Dora with her?'

'Yes, O lord and god.'

'I don't even know her name!' Juba heard the soft pad of footsteps and then the Emperor's voice right behind him.

'Boy!'

'Yes, O lord and god.' Juba remained in his kneeling position and turned to the Emperor, keeping his head down.

210

Domitian's voice was cold. 'It has just occurred to me. You and little Dora could almost be brother and sister.'

Juba kept his eyes on the marble floor. Domitian was wearing sandals and Juba could see his hammertoes.

'Look at me, boy!'

Juba fought to control his emotions. He could not let Domitian see his fear and loathing. He tried to make his face blank and raised his head as ordered.

He saw understanding spark in the Emperor's eyes.

'You're her older brother!' Domitian cried. 'I've been seeking you for years. You took the jewels and gems that were mine by rights! And Titus, my talking bird! You stole him, too! You are the son of Ursus, the merchant who sold all his treasures and left me nothing but the husk of his house!'

Juba saw the flush of anger turn Domitian's cheeks from pink to red. He had to say something.

'Material wealth is not important, O my lord and god.'

'What? You would quote Seneca at me? That tyrant-killer?'

'Princeps.' A man stood in the doorway.

It was sallow-skinned Parthenius. 'Your niece's steward Stephanus is here. He says he has a message of huge importance. Details of a clever plot against you.'

'Stephanus?' cried Domitian. 'Loyal steward of the niece I recently exiled? Do you think I can trust him?'

'Yes, Lord. Stephanus is not loyal to his mistress but to you. He has thwarted an assassination attempt and can give you the names of all the conspirators.'

Juba felt sick. The conspiracy had been uncovered! Someone had given up the names. And his must be on the list.

'Very well,' said Domitian after a short pause. 'Send him in. And fetch back little Dora and the girl who took her.'

No! Juba's heart was screaming.

Domitian turned to Juba and jabbed a finger at him. 'You wait right here.'

Heart pounding, Juba pressed his forehead to the cool marble floor.

What could he do? The plot had been exposed. He had an incriminating tattoo on his scalp. And guards were about to bring back Bouda and Dora.

There was only one thing for him to do.

Juba crawled to the chest upon which the shrine stood.

Earlier that morning he had taken the dagger from under Domitian's pillow and split its ivory handle with the heavy bronze base of one of the Minerva statues. He had removed the flanged blade and then stuck the two sides of the handle back together using candlewax. The handle was in the dagger sheath back under the Emperor's pillow, but the blade was wedged behind the chest.

Only it wasn't.

The dagger blade was not where he had hidden it.

'Help, boy!' came a sudden shout from the bedroom. And then a high-pitched scream.

Bouda! She had come back and was in trouble.

Heart pounding, Juba scrambled to the shrine's doorway.

But what he saw there stopped him cold.

Bouda was nowhere in sight. In the centre of the bedroom, two men were embracing: Domitian and a blond man with a bandaged forearm.

The Emperor's wig was half on and half off. His eyes bulged with terror.

Then Juba understood. They weren't embracing. They were struggling.

212

The blond man had a thin stiletto blade and was trying to stab the Emperor. He had already got him once: a dark red stain was blossoming at Domitian's groin.

'My dagger!' shrieked the Emperor. 'Boy! Get my dagger! Under my pillow!' The high-pitched scream had been his.

Juba stood frozen in horror. Then he ran to the bed, as if he didn't already know what he would find.

'Quick!' screeched Domitian. 'Quick!'

The Emperor had grasped the assassin's thin blade. Blood was dripping down his forearm.

Juba threw aside the pillow. 'I'm sorry, sir!' He held up the scabbard and the ivory handle. 'Someone has removed the blade!'

'Bring me something else!' squealed Domitian. 'Anything!'

Suddenly, the blond man slipped on the spreading pool of blood and fell on to his back. Juba heard the crack of his head on the marble floor. But he was still conscious as the Emperor straddled him and tried to gouge out his eyes.

'*Aieeee*!' screamed the blond man as Domitian dug bloody thumbs into the man's eye sockets.

Juba turned away in horror and ran back into the octagonal lararium.

He had always thought of himself as brave but this cold-blooded assassination was the most horrible thing he had ever witnessed. He knelt, trembling, before Minerva's shrine and tried to pray.

The shouts and screams from the bedroom changed tone, new voices had joined in.

Still on hands and knees, Juba scrabbled to the door of the shrine and peered out. Three more figures now crouched over Domitian. One was dressed as a gladiator. One was Maximus, the man who had brought Juba to the palace. And one was Satur, the Emperor's body slave. The handsome youth kept raising his fist and bringing it down.

Then Juba understood. Beautiful Satur had the missing dagger blade in his hand.

Chapter Forty
NERVA

It was late afternoon of Domitian's deathday, and the sun had just dropped behind the temple roofs. Ursula and Doctor Jonathan were still praying in the portico of the temple when a flutter of wings made Ursula look up.

'*Cave Domitian!*' said Loquax, settling on her shoulder.

'Loquax!' cried Ursula. And then, looking at the doctor. 'Is this bad? Or good?'

The answer came a moment later with the herald's distant shout.

'Did he just say what I thought he said?' Doctor Jonathan asked her.

'Yes!' whispered Ursula. 'He said Domitian is dead.'

A moment later a boy not much older than Ursula came running along the portico.

'Domitian is dead!' exulted the boy, slapping each column as he passed it. 'We have a new Emperor, an old man called Nerva!'

'*Cave Domitian!*' cried Loquax. Gartha was on her feet.

'Wait!' cried Jonathan as the boy rushed past.

The boy skidded to a halt. 'What?' he cried, his dark eyes shining with excitement.

'Do they know who did it?'

The boy nodded. 'A man named Stephanus, I think. Or maybe Maximus. And one of the Emperor's bedroom slaves.'

'Oh no!' hissed Ursula after the boy had gone. 'Do you think the bedroom slave was Juba? Shouldn't he and Bouda be back by now?'

Jonathan nodded grimly. 'If they've already announced a new Emperor then the assassination must have happened a few hours ago at least. You're right to be worried.'

'*Cave Domitian!*' cried Loquax, and Gartha whined.

'Oh, Doctor Jonathan!' Ursula cried. 'Can't you for once in your life be hopeful?'

'Yes,' he replied, gazing over her shoulder. 'Look.'

Ursula turned to see Bouda emerging from the entrance to the Palatine ramp. She held a squirming brown-skinned toddler in her arms.

'Bouda!' cried Ursula. 'And Dora! Oh, praise the Lord, Doctor Jonathan! She's found my little sister, Dora!'

Ursula ran forward to embrace her long-lost sister, but when she came closer she stopped. Bouda looked exhausted and her eyes were red from weeping.

'Tata!' cried toddler Dora, pushing against Bouda. 'Want Tata!'

'*Cave Domitian!*' said Loquax, perching on Ursula's head.

'Where's Juba?' Ursula looked over Bouda's shoulder.

'And who's Tata?' Doctor Jonathan gently took the squirming toddler from Bouda's exhausted arms.

'I don't know where Juba is!' sobbed Bouda. 'I was waiting for him in one of the alcoves of the tunnel, but I couldn't last any longer.' She looked at little Dora. 'Tata is Domitian. Dora thinks he's her father.'

216

Chapter Forty-One
DAMNATIO MEMORIAE

B ouda had never prayed so hard in her life.
She prayed to her own patron goddess, Minerva.

She prayed to Juba's special god, Mercury.

She prayed to Jupiter and Juno, Venus and Vulcan, Castor and Pollux. She even tried praying to the shepherd God of Doctor Jonathan and Ursula.

Doctor Jonathan said that a fast gave power to prayers, so for the next twelve hours none of them ate a bite except for little Dora and big Gartha, who finished off the last of the bread and cheese. While Bouda, Ursula and Jonathan prayed in the portico at the back of the Temple of Castor and Pollux, little Dora ran giggling after Gartha, who patiently endured the game and stayed close by. Dora no longer asked for Tata; she was besotted with the 'big puppy'. When it got dark the exhausted toddler finally curled up against Gartha's flank and slept.

Bouda woke at dawn the following day, just in time to see Juba emerge from the entrance to the ramp. He was escorted by two members of the Praetorian Guard but they left him in the growing light.

With a cry, Bouda ran to embrace him.

'Thank you, Minerva,' she whispered, and fought back tears as she hugged him.

'They interrogated me all night,' Juba told them a short time later in their shelter beneath the portico. 'But in the end the new Emperor let me go.'

Ursula looked at him with huge eyes. 'Did you help kill . . .?' she trailed off.

'No. But I saw it happen. It was terrible. So much blood. And it took him so long to die.' He glanced around. 'I'll tell you about it later, when we're out of Rome. I just want to get away.'

'Come.' Doctor Jonathan put a hand on Juba's shoulder. 'Let's have something to eat and then go back to Ostia. I know my mother will be happy to see me and to offer us shelter. Are you up to walking?'

Juba looked exhausted but he nodded. 'Oh and look!' He removed something from around his neck. 'Nerva said I could keep it.'

'The Minerva Gem!' cried Bouda, taking it. 'That reminds me. You need your little Mercury. The one you buried under the pine tree by your old house.'

They went around to the northeast side of the Palatine Hill and all drank at the fountain while Juba retrieved his lucky statuette.

When he emerged, Bouda saw him give his old front door one last look. Ursula looked, too, then buried her face in Gartha's fur and wept.

Presently she stopped and smiled and nodded. It was like the sun coming out from clouds and Bouda felt such a surge of love for Juba's sister that she gave her a long hug.

Then they turned and made their way south towards the Ostia Gate.

There was a spirit of festival in the forum. It was the first hour on the final day of popular games and Rome had a new Emperor. Food vendors were everywhere so they bought hot, spiced wine and roast chestnuts and ate them as they made their way along the sunny streets of Rome.

Dora had taken a liking to Juba, and insisted he carry her.

As they left the Sacred Way, Bouda saw some workmen smashing inscriptions and statues.

'What are they doing?' she asked Juba, who had just hoisted Dora on to his shoulders.

'*What ARE you doing?*' echoed Loquax, fluttering up into the air.

'*Damnatio memoriae*, I believe,' said Doctor Jonathan. 'Destruction of memory.'

Juba nodded. 'We've had ten Emperors since Augustus, some good and some bad. But Domitian is the first one whom the senate has voted to forget.'

'*Damnatio memoriae!*' confirmed Loquax, settling on Ursula's right shoulder.

Near the Arch of Titus, Bouda saw a man standing by a marble statue, using a chisel to transform Domitian's plump face into a thin one.

The sculptor was already on the final stages and they stopped to watch.

'Nerva,' said Juba after a moment. 'That's what our new Emperor looks like.'

'He looks old,' said Ursula.

'He is,' said Juba. 'When he questioned me he had a bad cough. He's not long for this world, I think. They say he's going to adopt Trajan to succeed him,' he added, with a significant look.

219

'The mastermind behind Domitian's assassination!' whispered Bouda.

Juba nodded.

'We must pray that Nerva and his successor will be wise emperors,' said Doctor Jonathan, leaning on his walking stick.

Behind them they heard jeers and whistles and then the bone-tingling screech of metal. They all turned to see Domitian's colossal bronze head topple behind temple roofs.

'Tata!' cried Dora, pointing at the disappearing head. 'Want Tata!'

Glumly, they resumed walking towards the Ostia Gate.

'Juba,' asked Bouda, as they passed the eastern end of the Circus Maximus, 'was Domitian really evil? He seemed so sad and lonely when I saw him.'

'I've been thinking about that,' said Juba. 'I don't think he was intentionally evil, but he was a bully. He was mean when he had power but pathetic when he was afraid. They say he used to stab flies on his stylus and then pick off their wings.'

'That's true,' said Doctor Jonathan. 'And I agree with your assessment. Like many bullies, he was self-obsessed and had no pity for others. If Domitian had been merely a butcher or a sailor he only would have made life miserable for his small circle of family and slaves. A man like that should not be given the power to rule an empire.'

Juba shot Bouda a sidelong glance. 'Do you know that after you and Dora left, when he thought the danger of assassination had passed, he became bold again and commanded that the two of you be seized and returned to him?'

'He did?'

Juba lowered Dora from his shoulders and held her to his

chest. 'If they hadn't killed him, we'd all three be his slaves. Or worse.'

Bouda shuddered.

A man on a small donkey trotted past. Dora looked after him and then pointed at Gartha. 'Me want to ride big puppy!' she cried.

They all laughed and Dora got her wish.

And so the five of them made their way through the rejoicing streets of Rome: Bouda and Juba, Ursula and Doctor Jonathan, and little Dora, happily riding Gartha as a child rides a pony.

'*Cave Domitian!*' observed Loquax suddenly from his perch on Ursula's shoulder.

'Not any more, praise Minerva,' whispered Bouda.

Juba took her hand and they continued southwest towards Ostia, and their new lives.

EPILOGUS

R ome was the Eternal City.
Bouda had dreamt of going there since she was little.

But now that she was in Italy, she preferred to live in Rome's port, Ostia. Although she had vowed never to set foot on a ship again, she liked being close to the sea. She loved the smell and sight of it. She enjoyed seeing people from all over the Roman Empire when she shopped in the Marina Forum. There, she saw Syrians, Gauls, Germans, Egyptians and of course Britons. Sometimes when she was shopping with little Dora she would hear someone speaking Brittonic. It always brought back a flood of memories. At those times she usually pulled her palla closer to hide her head. If they saw her copper hair they would want to talk about the past. And she preferred to live in the present.

She and Juba were married the year Trajan became Emperor, when she was fifteen and he was almost seventeen. Some of Juba's family fortunes had been restored and they were able to buy a small townhouse on Green Fountain Street. It had once been the childhood home of Flavia Gemina, their patroness. Juba's clients visited him here every morning. They would sit in his tablinum, smiled upon by a bust of Trajan, who was proving to be Rome's best and greatest Emperor.

222

While Juba received his clients, Bouda sat in the sunny inner garden and wove. From her hidden position she could hear what Juba said to his clients and what they said to him. Afterwards, over dinner, they would discuss his cases and he often asked for her advice. She helped him with his speeches, too, and always went to hear him when he defended a client in the basilica.

Old Avia had come to live with them and she was a loving presence for Dora and, later, Juba and Bouda's three children.

Bouda liked weaving in wool, because it reminded her of Britannia. It was easier and quicker than nettle-cloth and wool made a warmer cloak or tunic. But she always wove a lucky bolt of nettle-cloth in the spring, and gave it to Fronto.

Thanks to Trajan's patronage of Juba, Fronto and Vindex had been offered the choice jobs of Vigiles in Ostia. They put out fires and kept the night-time streets safe. Fronto and Bircha had four sons, handsome boys with creamy brown skin, dark eyes and flaxen hair. Vindex married a plump, dark-haired Ostian girl and they often came to dinner too.

Doctor Jonathan was still a travelling doctor, trying to save eighty thousand lives to bring an ancient crime into balance. Ursula became his assistant and together they travelled the Roman Empire, healing men, women, children and animals.

The twins, Castor and Raven, became gem merchants. Bouda suspected it was an excuse for them to sail the world. Their uncle had been a sea captain and they often joked that they had seawater in their veins.

Lupus and Clio settled in Ostia too. Now that philosophers and pantomime dancers were no longer illegal, it was safe for them to live in Italy. They had a girl and a boy, and when Flavia's husband died they bought a big townhouse across the street from Bouda and Juba and lived there with Flavia, Nubia, Aristo and their children.

As well as their own children, there were three orphans they had adopted. They called their massive townhouse the Villa Flavia and once a week they held morning meetings for followers of the new religion called the Way.

Sometimes, perhaps every three to five years, they were all home to celebrate a wedding or birth or one of their many festivals. If it were winter, they would gather in the Villa Flavia. If it were summer, they would meet at the house of Jonathan's mother, the opulent Villa Susannah, outside the town walls by the beach.

Bouda and Juba were prosperous, but she had learned not to put her trust in possessions. She only wore one piece of jewellery: an oval chrysolite with the goddess Minerva carved into its leaf-green face. It was her wedding ring.

Not long after she and Juba married, Bouda sold the Minerva gem and used the gold to set up a fund to help feed poor and orphaned children.

Although she was now a respectable Roman matron, she would sometimes wrap herself in a dark palla and explore the backstreets of Ostia and even Portus in search of lost or orphaned children. For Flavia Gemina was still her patroness, and Bouda would always be a Quester at heart.

FINIS

WHAT THE LATIN CHAPTER HEADERS MEAN

PROLOGUS – prologue
Opening to a story that establishes its setting.

1. GLADIATRIX – a female gladiator
    We have evidence of girl and women gladiators from Roman times, but not (as yet) of this word.

2. PATRONA – patroness
    A patron was a protector, defender and advisor; in return, his clients did favours for him. There were also some female patrons in Roman times.

3. OSCILLUM – hanging disc
    The word means anything that swings or revolves, but in this case it refers to a dangling pottery or marble garden ornament used to keep away birds and evil spirits.

4. NUNTIUS – messenger
    We get our word 'announcer' from Latin nuntio – 'I announce, bring a message'.

5. NUPTIAE – wedding
    The Latin word is linked to the word nubo, 'I cover' which also can mean 'I marry', because the bride is covered with a veil. The English word 'nuptials', meaning a marriage ceremony, comes from it.

6. NOX – night
    We get the word 'nocturnal' from the Latin word for night.

7. TABLINUM – study
The main room of a Roman house, originally used for writing, doing business and receiving clients.

8 ANIMALIA – animals
The Latin word for animal comes from the word anima, 'breath', because an animal is anything that has breath.

9. FAENUM – hay
In Roman times hay was often used as packing material.

10. BOVES – oxen
We get the word 'bovine' (cow-like) from the Latin word for cattle.

11. TORTOR – a torturer
The word comes from a root meaning to twist.

12. NAUSEA – sea-sickness
This word comes from the Greek word 'naus' which means 'ship', because you often feel sea-sick on board ship.

13. TEMPESTAS – storm
We get the word 'tempest' from the Latin word for storm.

14. GESORIACUM – Boulogne
In the time our story is set, this was the main port on the mainland connecting Europe to Britain.

15. TINCTA – dyed things
We get the word 'tint' from the Latin word for dye.

16. FLOCCI – tufts of wool
We get the word 'flock' from the Latin word for bits of wool.

17. COMAE – head of hair
    This word can also mean 'mane'. We get the word 'comet' from it because comets seem to have fiery hair streaming out behind them.

18. MORS – death
    We get the words 'mortal' and 'immortal' from the Latin word for death.

19. MONILE – necklace
    Some women kept their wealth in the form of jewellery.

20. TURPITUDO – disgrace
    This is a particularly unpleasant type of shame in which it is your own fault.

21. CALIGO – fog
    This word can mean a literal fog but also mental confusion or darkness.

22. COLONIA – Cologne
    A colonia or 'colony' was originally a Roman city of retired soldiers founded in a conquered area. Many Roman towns had this word in their official name but Köln (Cologne) in Germany is one of the few whose modern name still reflects that.

23. TRAIANUS – Trajan
    Trajan was Rome's thirteenth Emperor. Some scholars believe he might have been behind Domitian's assassination, though there is no documented proof of this.

24. FASCIAE – bandages
    Strips of cloth, usually linen, were used to bind up wounds.

25. INSIDIAE – plot
This word can also mean an ambush. We get the word 'insidious' (i.e. treacherous or cunning) from this word.

26. ODYSSEY – journey
The name of Homer's epic poem about the return home from Troy of the Greek hero Odysseus has come to mean a long journey in English.

27. AESTAS – summer
Sometimes this word meant the hot half of the year but the Romans usually had mid-June to mid-September in mind.

28. OSTIA – Ostia Antica
Rome's earlier seaport, 14 miles from Rome at the mouth of the River Tiber, was still in use even after a bigger harbour called Portus was built a few miles north about fifty years before this story takes place.

29. DOMINUS ET DEUS – 'Lord and god'
It is reported – but so far not confirmed – that Domitian asked his subjects to address him as 'god' near the end of his reign, a shocking thing to most Romans.

30. REDEMPTIO – redemption
To redeem or ransom was to 'buy back' something that was already yours, i.e. a kidnapped child.

31. EQUUS – horse
Although this word means 'horse' it was occasionally applied to an equestrian sculpture, i.e. a statue of a man on a horse.

32. CRYPTA – underground passage
    This word can also refer to a cave, vault or grotto. The word means anything 'hidden'.

33. CUBICULARIUS – bedroom slave
    From the word cubiculum, *'bedroom', this is the title of a slave or servant who attends to his master's toilet and dress.*

34. LARARIUM – shrine
    The lararium was a shrine to the 'Lares', minor deities who protected the house. They were usually shown as young men in fluttering tunics holding vessels for offerings. Other gods and goddesses might also be worshipped in the shrine.

35. PRECES – prayers
    A prayer is a request to a god or goddess for something.

36. PHENGITES – glittery rock
    This was a type of stone so shiny that you could see your reflection in it. Pliny the Elder mentions it twice in his Natural History.

37. MISERICORDIA – pity
    This word is made of two words, miser, *'wretched' and* cor, *'heart', with a sense of your heart aching for someone.*

38. PERSONA – mask
    We get the word 'personality' from the Latin word for mask.

39. CLADES – slaughter
    The Latin word can also mean defeat or ruin.

40. NERVA – Nerva
Nerva was the twelfth Emperor of Rome. Old and sickly, he ruled for less than two years before he was succeeded by his adopted son, Trajan.

41. DAMNATIO MEMORIAE – cursing of memory
This is the Roman practice of destroying images of a person and erasing references to them, to make it seem as if they had never existed.

EPILOGUS – epilogue
A short passage or chapter that briefly tells what happens after the main story and ties up loose ends.